# Why She Cries,
## I Do Not Know

# Why She Cries, I Do Not Know

## By WHIT MASTERSON

A Red Badge Novel of Suspense

DODD, MEAD & COMPANY

NEW YORK

ISBN: 0-396-06615-1
Library of Congress Catalog Card Number: 72-3142
Printed in the United States of America
by Vail-Ballou Press, Inc., Binghamton, N. Y.

*To our Sari and her Bob*
*with undivided love*

# Why She Cries,
## I Do Not Know

# One

THE ROOM WAS COLD, with a chill that was not entirely due to the refrigeration which kept the temperature a few degrees above freezing. The attendant wore a sweater beneath his white smock and still shivered. Those he attended wore considerably less but felt nothing.

"Sure you want to go through with this?" the deputy coroner asked. "It's not pretty and there's no real need. We've already established identification through fingerprints."

"Don't say 'it,' " the tall young man in rumpled khaki requested softly, an edge to his voice. "Say 'he.' And I do want to see him. The Army flew me damn near ten thousand miles so I could take a final look."

"Up to you," the deputy coroner agreed with a shrug. "Just keep in mind that a man who gets hit by a train . . . Open Number Five, Sammy."

The attendant selected one from among two dozen large drawers which lined the morgue like some giant filing cabinet. Number 5 slid out noiselessly on ball-bearing rollers to reveal its shrouded contents. The deputy coroner lifted the muslin sheet.

The young soldier stared down at what had once been a human face. He turned away suddenly, groping with both hands for the door. He stumbled through it, colliding with the jamb, and found support against the corridor wall.

"Well, you warned him," the attendant observed, closing the drawer with a clang. "You'd think he'd be used to seeing bodies, where he's been."

"There's one big difference," the deputy coroner told him. "Those were just bodies. This one's his brother."

Curtis Orr's funeral was sparsely attended. The mortuary chapel held a mere handful of mourners and the family alcove, screened from view by a gauze curtain, contained only one. The funeral director, a Mr. Hammond, hovered discreetly in the rear of the alcove, ready with sympathy and smelling salts.

Fletcher Orr—called Fletch by most—needed neither. He had received the news of the accident with shock and sorrow. By now the shock had faded. The sorrow remained but he could live with it, having no other choice, and present to the world a face devoid of tears. Curt would have wished him to do so, he knew. Curt, a thoroughgoing sentimentalist who prided himself in concealing it, would have derided an outward show of grief. *Snap out of it, kid, and act like a man . . .*

Curt himself had never been permitted to act otherwise. Orphaned while still in his teens, he had shouldered the responsibility not only for his own survival but for the survival of the brother five years his junior. The role of surrogate father had not been an easy one, Fletch realized. Curt must often have despaired as do all fathers, surrogate or natural, at the boy so different from himself. Curt was a doer who plunged wholeheartedly into any project, large or small, which roused his interest. Fletch was a drifter, charming and glib, who lived by his wits and felt no necessity to Make Something of Himself simply because the world expected it. When asked his occupation, he usually put down "actor" and there was some truth to this—but the greater truth was that he was a compulsive role-player. Curt had never understood his delight in inventing and making credible a character, any character, other than his

2

own, the extent of the masquerade limited only by his imagination and the gullibility of his audience. To Curt's no-nonsense mind, this smacked of knavery . . . and it was probable that Fletch could have made his fortune by relieving others of theirs. The fact that he did not choose to do so had not prevented Curt from accusing him of it and from predicting that he would come to a bad end.

Yet between the brothers, dissimilar in nearly every respect, had existed a strong and abiding love—and Fletch knew that death, capricious as always, had taken the better of the two. Curt had been his family, virtually the only family he could remember. Though he sat composed and dry-eyed, inwardly he raged at the fate which had separated them. But anger was no more productive than anguish; Curt was dead and there was nothing he could do about it.

The service was brief. An organist played, a soloist sang and a clergyman, supplied by the mortuary and unacquainted with the deceased, spoke the traditional words of scriptural comfort. Afterward, three or four of the mourners came forward to stand for a moment beside the closed casket. Fletch recognized none of them and only one aroused his interest. She appeared out of place there, a petite young woman (nineteen, he guessed, possibly twenty) with blond hair which flowed down her back, dressed more for a picnic than a funeral in a floppy white shirt and frayed denim jeans. She was the last to approach the bier and remained the longest, head bowed pensively. Before turning away, she placed a single rose delicately upon the casket as if bestowing a benediction.

Fletch watched her depart, unable to imagine under what circumstances she had known his brother. Curt's letters had not mentioned any romance and she hardly seemed his type in any case. There was no one to satisfy his curiosity. The young woman was already gone and so too, in a more permanent sense, was Curt.

He dismissed her from his mind and asked Mr. Hammond, "Well, what now?"

The funeral director cleared his throat uneasily. "You're welcome to wait here—or to come back after lunch if you'd rather. That is, unless you've changed your mind and would prefer that we handle the arrangements. I really think, Mr. Orr—"

"Is there any law which says I can't scatter Curt's ashes personally?"

"Certainly not. The only legal stipulation is that the burial must be at sea at least three miles from shore. Here in Southern California, we're conducting this type of, ah, disposal at the rate of thirty per day."

"Then what's the objection?"

"I hope you don't think it has anything to do with money. Our fee—including the aircraft—is the same either way. It's just a bit unusual, that's all. Most people would find it, well, awkward. But if that's what you wish . . ." Mr. Hammond's tone was disapproving. There was an established funerary ritual in which both bereaved and mortician played clearly defined roles, the one to grieve passively while the other attended to the practical mechanics. Fletch's usurpation of his role plainly piqued him.

"That's what I wish." He had loved Curt too much to surrender him to impersonal hands for his final journey. The task might be painful—and no one would blame him for shirking it—but in him was a fierce desire to pay this last slight homage to his brother. He felt no need to justify himself to outsiders. It was between him and Curt, and Curt would have understood. But since Mr. Hammond obviously did not, Fletch felt it better not to disturb him further by remaining underfoot. "I will come back later, though, whenever you say."

Mr. Hammond looked relieved, as if he had feared Fletch might also insist upon assisting in the cremation.

4

"Would two o'clock be convenient? Our regular flight is scheduled for three-fifteen so that should give you plenty of time to reach the airport without taking chances on the freeway." The matter settled, he even attempted a pallid joke. "We don't need any more customers, you know."

Fletch picked up the solitary rose from atop the casket as he left the chapel. He was still carrying it when he returned at two o'clock that afternoon to receive another burden only slightly heavier. Curt Orr had been a big man, larger than his brother who stood an even six feet and weighed one hundred and seventy-five pounds. Yet all that remained of him now was easily contained in a black leather satchel the size of a woman's handbag. The satchel, Mr. Hammond cautioned, was to be retained and returned. Only the inner lining, an ordinary brown paper bag, was to be cast adrift high above the Pacific Ocean.

The ride to the Burbank airport, through the smog-choked city and across the overbuilt hills, was long and melancholy. The mortuary limousine was designed to hold nine passengers. Fletch, seated in the rear, felt lost in it. He had ridden a hearse only once before, many years ago at his parents' funeral, and then Curt had ridden beside him. He tried to imagine it was Curt sitting beside him now, and failed. The satchel did not contain the man, only his powdery residue. I won't forget you, Fletch vowed; it was all he had to offer.

The limousine deposited him and the satchel at the airport terminal. The driver directed him to the charter service employed by the mortuary and offered to await his return. Fletch dismissed him with thanks. He did not know how he would spend the remaining twenty-four hours of his leave, where he could go or how he might get there. It didn't bother him. From the moment of his arrival in Los Angeles two days ago, there had been officials to see, forms to complete and arrangements to make. He looked forward to being alone, free from the world's sympathy as well as its questions.

He discovered shortly that he had not yet achieved that freedom. The charter aircraft was waiting on the apron adjacent to the terminal, engines idling. When he reached it, Fletch saw to his surprise that the small cabin already contained another passenger. He was a man of seventy—but a vigorous seventy—with snow-white hair and a bushy mustache the same color in sharp contrast to the florid face. The wrinkled skin of his throat and hands seemed too large for the flesh it covered, as if its wearer had been partially deflated.

"Yes, you have the right plane," he said, interpreting Fletch's hesitation correctly. His bony handshake was surprisingly strong. "How do you do, Mr. Orr. I'm Henry Sugarman."

The name meant nothing but Fletch felt he had seen its owner before. After an instant, he remembered where. "You were at the funeral, weren't you? Sitting toward the back."

"The last row," Sugarman agreed. "You have both good observation and a good memory." He sounded pleased, although Fletch could not imagine why. "Your brother and I were friends. I'd like to fly along with you if you don't mind."

Fletch shook his head slowly. "I'm afraid I do mind. I don't mean to seem rude. I appreciate the offer. But this is, well, call it a family affair. I really don't want company." He moved aside to allow the other man to depart.

Sugarman did not move. "It's not a frivolous request. In fact, you might say it's not actually a request at all." He smiled slightly.

"I don't know what you're getting at but the answer is still no, Mr. Sugarman."

"General Sugarman," the old man corrected him. "I hate to pull rank on you, son, especially at a time like this. So why don't you make it easier on both of us by inviting me to go along?"

Outraged indignation rose in Fletch, robbing him of speech. It was just as well; all at once the absurdity of the situation struck him, dissolving his anger. "Yes, sir!" he said and gave Sugarman an exaggerated salute. "Welcome aboard, General."

"Thank you," Sugarman murmured, unruffled by the sarcasm. "I felt sure you'd see it my way." A moment later he added, "Oh, by the way—at ease, soldier."

# Two

THE AIRPLANE TAXIED out to the runway, took off and turned west across the mountains toward the sea. Sugarman did not speak again until they reached their assigned altitude and the engine roar had subsided to a comfortable purr. "Now then," he said briskly, "suppose we begin."

"Begin what, General?"

"Our discussion. Why else did you think I'm here?"

"You said you were Curt's friend. I assumed that—"

"Funerals are a waste of time. Worse than that, they're an exercise in masochism that does no one any good. Curt knew how I felt about him because I told him while he was alive. Consequently, I consider public breast-beating unnecessary. I attended simply because I wanted to talk with you. I thought I might get that opportunity at the mortuary—but when I learned you were making this flight it seemed even more suitable. We can talk here without interruption." He gestured at the pilot who, though only a half-dozen feet away on the flight deck, could neither see nor hear his passengers.

Fletch regarded him with mystification. "Pardon me, sir—but do you mind telling me just what the hell you're selling?"

"I'll get to that presently. First, though, let me congratulate you on a successful combat tour. Helicopters, wasn't it?"

"Med-Evac. Fletcher the Stretcher Fetcher, that's me.

But as far as combat goes, my orders were to avoid it and I'm proud to say I obeyed them to the letter."

"Bronze Star, Purple Heart, Air Medal with a half-dozen clusters—they suggest otherwise."

"Don't let gift wrap fool you, General. There's no hero inside. The biggest battle I fought was to keep from getting drafted—and I lost that one. After that, all I did can be summed up in two words: I survived." Fletch held up crossed fingers. "So far. I still owe Uncle six more stinking weeks."

"Have it your own way," Sugarman murmured. "Forget the past. Let's talk about the future. Assuming you go the distance, what are your plans for afterward?"

Fletch sighed. "Ordinarily I don't mind talking about myself because I'm my favorite subject. But not today. If you'd like to rap about Curt—"

"I'm not making idle conversation, Orr. What do you intend to do once you're back in the world?"

"To tell you the truth, I haven't thought much about it," Fletch replied snappishly. "Pick up where I left off, I guess."

"Show business, you mean? That may not be so easy. In case you haven't heard, Hollywood's in deep trouble. Fewer pictures being made, runaway production, a cutback in television . . . The market's glutted with unemployed actors these days. You find them parking cars and washing dishes just to stay alive. And you've been away two years. Don't expect any banners saying 'Welcome back, Chris Fletcher!'" Sugarman eyed him curiously. "Why did you find it necessary to change your name, by the way?"

"I got tired of telling agents and casting directors 'I'm Fletcher Orr' and having them come back with 'Or what?'" Fletch shrugged. "Okay, so times are rough. I made it once. I can make it again."

Sugarman's eyebrows rose skeptically. "A handful of

minor roles in TV, one sixty-second commercial and two industrial training films—is that your definition of making it?"

"Curt must have really shot his mouth off about me," Fletch said slowly.

"On the contrary. The only thing I ever recall Curt saying was that he considered you the greatest con artist of our times. The rest of what I know about you comes from my own research which, I don't mind saying, has been quite thorough."

"Then how come you overlooked my best credit? Just before the Army grabbed me I had the starring role in a nifty little feature called—"

"*Kiss Me or Kill Me.* I've seen it so you can skip the buildup. I agree with the critic who said it was a shame there was an ordinance forbidding the burning of trash. Your performance was the best thing about it but that isn't saying much."

Fletch chuckled. "Okay, it was a turkey. But now that we're letting our hair down, I didn't think much of your last war, either."

"I take it that you have the same opinion of generals that I have of actors."

"One thing you can say for actors. When we bomb, we don't kill anybody."

"Would your prejudice prevent your working for one?" The bushy mustache twitched in a slight smile. "By the way, I'm retired, if that makes any difference."

"Is that what this is all about?" Fletch asked incredulously. "You're offering me a job? Doing what?"

"Acting. Pretending to be something you aren't. From what I understand, you do that even better off-screen than on."

"Don't tell me. You're actually the head of the CIA and you're seeking a man to substitute for Herman, Crown Prince of Provolone, who has been abducted by the evil

Archduke Irving. I happen to be a dead ringer for the missing prince, so consequently—"

"If that were even remotely true, would you be interested?"

"No. Not just no but hell, no!"

"Good," Sugarman said. "I have no use for romantics. We don't live in a romantic world any longer, more's the pity. It's the age of realism. We've replaced the swashbuckler with a computer. The grand gesture is passé. Worse than that, it's camp. I suppose that's the price we pay for sophistication. I regret it but I accept it."

"Should I be taking notes, General? I have the feeling you're going to ask questions later."

"On the other hand," Sugarman continued, ignoring the sarcasm, "sophistication hasn't robbed us of all the old-fashioned virtues. They still exist, though in smaller quantities. Patriotism, for instance. How do you feel about this country, Orr?"

"What kind of an answer are you looking for, General? If you mean, do I get a lump in my throat when they play the national anthem, I don't. If you mean, is my motto 'My country, right or wrong,' it isn't. We've blown it more than somewhat the past few years with that kind of knee-jerk reflex. But if you mean, would I still rather be an American than anything else, I would. Shall I go on?"

"Please do."

"Okay, you asked for it. I don't believe that all wars are immoral but I do believe that most are unnecessary and I can't see dying for the sake of Mom's apple pie—because she made a lousy crust. I don't badmouth hardhats. Times the past year when I was damn glad to wear one myself. By the same token, I don't consider long hair immoral, hard rock degenerate or draft resisters traitors. I don't blame your generation for all the world's troubles and I don't expect my generation is going to solve them all. I'm not sure whether that makes me a radical conservative or a conservative radical and I don't much care." Fletch smiled wryly. "And if you can get all that on a bumper sticker, I'll take a dozen."

"Let me try. Would a fair summation be that, while you think the United States is far from perfect, you're willing to work for change within our existing political structure?"

"Depends on how you define working. I hate to admit it after that rousing speech but politics don't really grab me."

"They grabbed your brother. Strongly."

"Curt had his thing, I have mine. He was always into some cause or other. Start a crusade and he was ready to march. Me, I'm the type who asks, 'Is this trip necessary?' "

"Perhaps I could persuade you to have a go at Curt's thing, as you put it," Sugarman suggested. "That job I mentioned—it was his."

"You mean Curt worked for you? Funny, he never mentioned it to me."

"He joined us shortly after you went overseas. He didn't tell you about it because he was ordered not to tell anyone. His value to COIN was in direct proportion to the fewer number of people who knew of the connection. On the surface, he continued to maintain his law office in Burbank but—"

"Wait a minute," Fletch interrupted. "What's COIN, anyway?"

"You mean you've never heard of us? I'm surprised. We've been rather well publicized, despite all I could do to prevent it. The name's an acronym—for Counter-Insurgency. We borrowed the term from the military but we're actually a civilian task force, organized and funded by a group of concerned private citizens for the purpose of counteracting subversive elements here at home. Our head-quarters is located out in the San Fernando Valley but that's just the tip of the iceberg. Our real work is done in the field."

" 'Counteracting subversive elements,' " Fletch repeated with a frown. "I thought that was what we pay the FBI for."

"It is. But it's a big job. We try to make it easier for them. Ours is a volunteer effort, like the Red Cross."

"Or the Ku Klux Klan."

"Oh, don't be ridiculous," Sugarman replied impatiently. "We're not vigilantes. Our function is to gather information, evaluate it and pass along our conclusions to the duly constituted authorities. What happens after that is up to them."

"And who are these so-called subversive elements? Anyone who doesn't happen to share your own political philosophy?"

"I call subversive anyone who is committed to the violent overthrow of the government. Case in point—the urban guerrilla coalition." He took notice of Fletch's blank expression and sighed. "Don't you get any news over there? Well, briefly, the urban guerrillas represent the lunatic fringe of the student protest movement, hardcore radical activists who have left the campus for a new battleground, the city. Their main weapon is terror, selectively used to disrupt, demoralize and ultimately destroy the society. COIN's mission is to prevent them from doing so."

"That has a nice stirring ring," Fletch scoffed. "But do you expect me to believe a bunch of spaced-out freaks constitute a real menace? Come off it, General."

"There's something so comforting about labels, isn't there? You should know better than to be seduced by them. Did calling the North Vietnamese dinks and slopeheads make them any less dangerous? By the same token, calling the urban guerrillas freaks doesn't diminish their potential for harm. I'll admit that they're still small in number—but even cancer begins with a single cell."

Fletch sighed. "Maybe you're right, maybe not. Either

way, why should I get involved?"

"You are involved. All of us are. The urban guerrillas are your enemy as much as mine. The real question is: Are you willing to fight them? I can give you two good reasons why your answer should be yes. First, you're a young man who obviously cares something about his country. Second, you're extremely well qualified—I might even say uniquely qualified—for the role." He hesitated. "There's a third reason also—but I hope that you'll consider the first two sufficient."

"You con pretty good, General," Fletch said slowly. "And that's praise from an expert. Uniquely qualified, am I? I'd like that in writing. There are a lot of people in this town who don't think I'm qualified for any role at all."

"Let me tell you what this particular role amounts to and you'll see what I mean." Sugarman gazed out the window at the wispy clouds drifting past the wingtip of the airplane, eyes narrowed as if contemplating a battlefield. He was, but it lay far beneath them, out of sight. "I mentioned that COIN has its headquarters here. So does the guerrilla coalition. Los Angeles is their nerve center. Until recently, it was controlled by a man named Bruno Sledge who holds the post of prime minister in the coalition's shadow cabinet. Sledge is currently on trial for murder in connection with the bombing of the federal building. Three people were killed, one of them a child. It wasn't Sledge's first murder. The difference is that this time we can prove it."

"So what's your problem?"

"Removing Sledge from circulation has crippled the guerrillas to some degree but it hasn't put them out of business by any means. They've been regrouping the past few months. We have reason to believe that they're getting ready for more mischief. Exactly what, we haven't been able to learn. It's essential that we do, and quickly." Sugarman removed his gaze from the window and turned it on his companion. "We need a man to penetrate their organization, worm his way into their confidence and find out what they're planning so we can prevent it."

Fletch winced. "You wouldn't be considering me for the part, would you?"

"The man I have in mind must be an actor—and a bit of a con artist besides, someone who can extemporize a character and make it hold up, come hell or high water. He must be young. And, finally, he must have no prior connection with COIN. I'd say that description fits you like a glove."

"You know what I say? No, thanks! Why, a man could get hurt doing what you're suggesting."

"Certainly, it's dangerous. But no more so than what you've been through the past year."

"That's just the point. I've already fought my war. Let somebody else fight this one."

Sugarman pursed his lips. "I've given you two good reasons why you're the man for the job. I mentioned that there was a third reason."

Before he could elaborate, the pilot stuck his head around the edge of the door to the flight deck. "This is it!" he called, pointing downward. "Use the starboard window—it slides toward you."

Fletch opened the satchel and removed the brown paper bag; it bore his brother's name in black grease pencil, like a schoolboy's lunch. He opened the window beside his right shoulder. The slipstream buffeted the bag, eager to wrench it from his fingers. He held on to it tightly for a moment longer, reluctant to sever the last fragile link to the past. Finally he relaxed his grasp. The bag vanished; before he could close the window it had disintegrated under the wind's violence. Nothing visible remained to indicate that it—or its contents—had ever existed.

Mission accomplished, the aircraft banked sharply, heading back the way they had come. Fletch stared down at the shimmering blue ocean five thousand feet beneath them as if to fix the spot forever in his memory. "Rest in peace, Curt," he said softly.

Sugarman cleared his throat. "That's the third reason —so that Curt may truly rest in peace."

"What are you talking about, General?"

"Call it retribution. You see, your brother's death wasn't an accident, the way you've been led to believe. Those people I've been telling you about—that bunch of spaced-out freaks—they murdered him."

# Three

*Dear Fletch,*

*I'm writing this letter in case something should happen to me. Doesn't that sound melodramatic, though? The truth is that your super-square brother has been leading a pretty melodramatic life recently. (Maybe some of your love of make-believe rubbed off on me, after all!) After you went overseas I decided I'd better do my bit too—couldn't let the kid get ahead of me, you know—and when the military wouldn't take me, I joined an organization called COIN, a sort of volunteer fire brigade that's trying to keep the old homestead from burning down. Up till now, all they've let me handle is office work—evaluating reports, drawing up position papers, that sort of thing —but I've finally convinced the General to give me an operational assignment.*

"What does he mean by 'operational assignment'?"

"Undercover work."

"My God!" Fletch groaned. "You must be out of your mind. Curt couldn't con a kitten with a saucer of cream."

"He was the only man I had available who met the physical requirements. The opportunity was too good to pass up."

*We've been trying for months to infiltrate the urban guerrilla organization here in L.A. Now, by a stroke of good luck, we've got the chance to put a man right in the middle of it and I'm that man. I won't go into all the sordid details—it's late, I'm bushed and they don't matter anyway—but suffice it to say that I look like somebody else, at least enough to get by (or so I hope!). I refuse to believe that you have all the acting talent in the Orr family.*

"Curt's look-alike was an older man—at least by guer-rilla standards—a courier from back East that the locals were expecting. We arranged for a delay en route to give Curt a chance to take his place for a few days. Nearly worked, too. According to the one report he filed, he was accepted almost without question."

"What went wrong?"

"The courier got away from us. I tried to recall Curt immediately but I couldn't reach him in time."

*I suppose if I had any sense I should be scared as hell but for some reason I'm not. The General thinks they might give me a rough time if they find out who and what I really am. I figure they'll either buy my act or they won't. If they do, fine. If they don't, about the worst that can happen is that they'll slam the door in my face. These kids aren't the Mafia—or even your old buddies, the V.C.*

"Curt made the worst mistake a soldier can make," Sug-arman said sadly. "He underestimated his enemy. He re-fused to believe that they were capable of killing him."

"How can you be sure they did? The police report said his car stalled on the tracks."

"Earlier that evening I received a railroad timetable with the nine P.M. train to San Diego underlined in red. It was that train which struck your brother's car. In the absence of other evidence, the police were compelled to write off Curt's death as an accident. I know it was an execution.

The guerrillas made sure I'd know by sending me the timetable."

*So that's about it. Reading over what I've written, I have half a mind to tear it up. But I guess I'll keep it. Maybe I'll show it to you sometime when we've hoisted a few too many. You can tell me how you played soldier and I can tell you how I played spy and we can both have a good laugh. Affectionately,*
Curt.
*P.S. Have I ever told you that I love you? Well, I do.*

Tears trickled down Fletch's cheeks; he blinked them away without shame. "Oh, God—why?" he asked huskily. "Why should anyone kill Curt, of all people? He never hurt a soul in his life."

"It was an object lesson. COIN has been giving the guerrillas a hard time recently. This was their way of warning us to lay off."

"You keep saying 'they.' That's not good enough. Name names."

"If you mean who actually put your brother in front of the train, I simply don't know. I am reasonably sure who gave the order. A chap named Lionel Gann, one of the top men in the guerrilla coalition."

"Then why hasn't this Gann been arrested?"

Sugarman shrugged. "Being reasonably sure of something and proving it are two different matters. We don't have a case against Gann that a jury would accept. Even if we did, arresting him at this time would be counterproductive. By waiting for the proper moment, we may be able to stamp out the whole scurvy crew."

"To hell with your proof—and to hell with your waiting, too. I'm going after Gann. He'll get the same kind of justice he gave Curt."

"I understand how you feel but taking the law into your own hands isn't the solution. Murder for revenge is still murder. We've got to submit ourselves to the discipline of due process, galling though it may be. Otherwise, we're no better than the scum we're fighting."

"I don't give a damn about proving my moral superiority. When somebody hits me, I hit back. It's as simple as that."

"I'm offering you the opportunity to hit back by finishing the job your brother started. Help us win this dirty little war—that's the vengeance Curt would have wanted."

"I don't know what Curt would have wanted and neither do you. I'll have to play this my way."

"Let me put it to you bluntly, Orr. You'll either play it my way or you won't play at all. That's not a threat, merely a statement of fact. Before you can deal with Lionel Gann you're going to have to find him and I'm the only one who can tell you where to look."

Fletch regarded him balefully. "I know my way around L.A. I'll find him."

"Take a look down there." Sugarman gestured at the earth beneath them. "That's home for close to five million people. Out of that number you've got to locate just one, a man you've never met and wouldn't recognize if you did. And on top of that, a man who is doing his damnedest to stay out of sight. Without my help, your hair will be as white as mine before you catch up with Lionel Gann, if you ever do." He hesitated, eyes narrowing. "But perhaps that's what you want, secretly. To strike the pose of the avenging brother while at the same time making sure that you don't have to put your money where your mouth is."

Fletch's voice rasped with anger. "You calling me a coward, General?"

"No—because I don't believe you are. You are an actor, a dealer in counterfeit emotions. You grit your teeth and tell me how you're determined to get Curt's killer. But when you refuse to do what it takes to get him, I can't help but wonder who's talking—the brother or the actor. I suggest you ask yourself the same question."

There was a grinding sound as the flaps were lowered; the plane shuddered and commenced to sink, losing airspeed. "Final appoach," Sugarman judged. He added with a wry smile, "And just in time to keep you from striking an old man and a superior officer, I'd say. Take a little while and cool down. I'll be in the restaurant across the street from the terminal. If you'd care to continue our conversation, I'll buy you a cup of coffee. If you haven't shown up in, say, fifteen minutes I'll assume that you prefer to buy your own coffee."

The restaurant was virtually deserted; the luncheon crowd had long since departed and the supper trade was yet to arrive. A few customers sat at the bar, grimly determined to take advantage of the late afternoon happy hour. Only the bartender appeared to be enjoying himself, however.

He brought a carafe of coffee to the dimly lit booth in the rear, collected the exorbitant price and departed, whistling. Sugarman poured two cups and watched enviously as Fletch added sugar and cream to his. He dropped two tiny white pills into his own. "It doesn't seem right," he said with a grimace. "That somebody named Sugarman should be restricted to saccharin. Always had a terrible sweet tooth, too, still have. But I've got to watch my blood pressure. Nothing better than a coronary to convince a man of that—except maybe the second one."

Fletch understood now the significance of the gaunt figure, the florid cheeks and, above all, the air of barely controlled impatience. The general was a man with a mission who feared he lacked the time in which to complete it. "Seems to me you should be taking life easier, sir."

"I'm a cavalryman, Orr. I rode a horse for Pershing and a tank for Patton. Damned if I intend to finish up in a rocking chair." The subject annoyed him. He dismissed it with a scowl and pushed a photograph across the table toward his companion. "Never mind me. Do you recognize her?"

"No. Wait a minute—she does seem familiar." Fletch snapped his fingers. "At the mortuary. That hippie type, the one who left the rose."

"Good boy," Sugarman said approvingly. "Do you think she saw you?"

"I doubt it. I was on the other side of the scrim and she didn't even look my way. Does it matter?"

"It does. That girl is your lead to Lionel Gann, the only lead we've got."

"You mean she's one of the guerrillas? My God, she's just a child!"

"She's younger than most. The average is around twenty-four or twenty-five. Your age. Timmy's barely nineteen."

"Timmy?"

"For Timothea. She's Ansel Towne's daughter." He watched Fletch's expression expectantly. When it didn't change, he said, "I thought everyone around L.A. knew Ansel Towne. He owns a large piece of it. You'll find the Towne brand on everything from real estate to race horses. And, ironically enough, it's largely Towne money which supports COIN."

"I don't get it. What's a millionaire's daughter doing skinny dipping in a cesspool?"

"It's not as unusual as you may suppose. By and large, the guerrillas are the product of affluence, not poverty. They're the kids who have had it all, the most unlikely bunch of anarchists in history. I don't pretend to understand what makes them tick and, quite frankly, I don't give a damn. I'm a soldier, not a sociologist. Let somebody else analyze them. My job is to eliminate them."

"How does Ansel Towne feel about your using his money against his own flesh and blood?"

"Towne hasn't spoken to his daughter in over a year. From what I gather, it's been a lot longer than that since there was any real communication between them." Sugarman shrugged. "Timmy was only nine when her mother died. Towne has had three wives since then. It's not what you call a close family relationship."

"The poor little rich girl, huh?"

"I'm sure that's how she sees herself. However, I don't feel sorry for her and I strongly recommend that you don't either. Never forget that she's your enemy. Keep that in mind if you want to stay alive."

Fletch studied the pretty young face in the photograph. Despite Sugarman's warning, he could not accept this innocent-appearing creature as an implacable foe. But then another face, mangled beyond recognition, intruded in his memory and he recalled that Curt had committed the same error. "You said she was my lead to Gann. Does that mean she had a hand in murdering my brother?"

"We know that Timmy recently joined Lionel Gann's cell and that Curt met her there. She may not have participated actively in the execution but she must have concurred with the sentence."

Fletch frowned. "If that's true, why on earth did she come to the services today?"

"For kicks, I suppose. We're dealing with warped minds, Orr. You can't expect them to behave like normal human beings."

Fletch's hand closed convulsively on the photograph, crushing the smiling face. "She put a rose on Curt's coffin," he said through clenched teeth. "Maybe I can return the favor."

"I gave you one piece of advice—don't feel sorry for Timmy. Now I'll give you another. Don't hate her, either."

"Why the hell not?"

"Because hatred is difficult to conceal, particularly from

a woman. Where emotions are concerned, they function at a gut level. A man can seduce a woman he doesn't love. It happens all the time. But I doubt if any man—even an actor—can seduce a woman he hates."

"Seduce?" Fletch echoed. "Are you saying I'm suppose to diddle the doll?"

"I see Timmy as the weak link in Gann's circle. She's his newest recruit, the youngest, the most vulnerable. Your job is to convince her to take you to him. Handle it any way you choose—but I suggest that an ounce of seduction might be worth more than several pounds of any other kind of persuasion."

"How far do you think I should go?"

"Good God, man!" Sugarman replied with good-natured exasperation. "As far as you have to, of course. What sort of a question is that?"

"A pretty stupid one, I guess." Fletch smoothed out the crumpled photograph and stared intently at its subject like a sculptor appraising a block of marble—or a leopard selecting its prey. "Okay, General, I'll take your suggestion. But how it plays depends on the lady. I may not be her type."

"You're young, handsome and oozing with charm. How could any girl possibly resist you?"

"I've often wondered about that myself." Fletch chuckled grimly. "Let's hope that Miss Timothea Towne doesn't come up with the answer."

# Four

HIS ORDERS DIRECTED him to return to duty with the Far East Asia Command via military air transport. However, the flight he boarded the next day was a commercial carrier and it took him no farther than San Francisco. Forty-eight hours later, he walked out of the Presidio, a civilian once more, to enter another—but no less dangerous—service. His discharge stated that he was being separated for the convenience of the government. A more accurate reason would have been for the convenience of the general. Sugarman, anxious for Fletch to take up his new assignment, had pulled strings to gain his early release.

"Six weeks short," the discharging officer commented with some amazement. "How'd you manage that, Orr?"

"National emergency, sir. The birth rate's falling and the Army figured I was more valuable on the home front."

The officer grinned. "Bet you can hardly wait to get started. But have a heart—leave a little work for the rest of us."

To judge by his actions, Fletch was in no hurry to begin that job, or any other. Though free to hasten back to Los Angeles, he remained in the bay city another week. He spent two days at the public library, reading everything available on the guerrilla movement. At night he pored over the biographies supplied by Sugarman until he knew them nearly as well as he knew his own. He allowed his beard to grow and purchased a new wardrobe from a thrift shop, replacing the mod with the odd. Suitably attired, he wandered the North Beach area, absorbing the feel of the counterculture which flourished there, steeping himself in its mystique and brushing up on its argot. Later, he crossed the bridge to Berkeley, there to tour the huge campus of the troubled university, notebook in hand, like an anthropologist studying some exotic civilization. An uninformed observer would have been hard put to fathom his behavior. A fellow actor would have had no difficulty at all: He was getting up in his part.

When, on the seventh day, he was offered narcotics in a coffee house, invited to join a political action group and stopped for questioning by a police officer, Fletch judged that he was ready. He bought a ten-year-old Volkswagen bus—shabby to behold but in sound mechanical condition—which had been outfitted as a camper by its previous owner. He registered the vehicle to Chris Fletcher, his professional name and the one he had chosen to use for the masquerade. He considered it highly unlikely that the guerrillas would recognize it when even those in the movie colony did not.

He drove south, eschewing the freeway for the tortuously winding coastal route. The scenic highway was heavily populated with hitchhikers, all of them young and many of them female. Fletch picked up as many as the bus would hold in order to practice his new identity before a critical, but not hostile, audience. Most were runaways, the girls particularly, but few had a destination; simply to be on the move to somewhere, anywhere, seemed to be enough for them. They drifted north or south depending on the season and their whims, searching for a dream none could define. They accepted Fletch as another drifter like themselves, never suspecting that he belonged to a world they characterized scornfully as "straight." By and large, he found them a pathetic lot, self-condemned to limbo. He reminded himself not to extend this judgment to the enemy he was soon to face. Though their life style resembled that of the nomads, the guerrillas were made of sterner stuff. The knowledge did not intimidate him. Vengeance aside, he relished the challenge as a test of his artistry.

He arrived in Los Angeles two weeks to the day following his brother's funeral, wearing a different sort of uniform, confident that he was fully prepared, mentally as well as physically, to settle the score with the guerrilla army, its leader Lionel Gann . . . and the girl called Timmy.

Fletch parked in a loading zone on Alvarado Street across from MacArthur Park, propped a book open on the steering wheel and pretended to read. His roving gaze found its target almost immediately among the predominantly elderly and uniformly nondescript throng to whom the two-block-square park was an oasis amid the urban desert. On weekends children scampered whooping over the grass and lovers rowed on the man-made lake. But this weekday afternoon most of the visitors sat somnolently on the benches or sprawled on the lawns, faces shielded by newspapers. Around them, on walks and boulevards, coursed a ceaseless stream of pedestrian and vehicular traffic, presumably with some destination.

Timmy Towne differed from the others in that she sought neither refuge nor relaxation. The park was her place of business. She drifted about its periphery with apparent aimlessness but Fletch, who had watched her on the previous afternoon also, recognized that she was, in fact, patrolling a beat. The child of affluence had become a sidewalk beggar.

She was costumed for the part. Timmy was clothed in patched jeans, a baggy shirt and a tattered poncho. She wore no shoes on her feet or makeup on her face. The blond hair which tumbled about her shoulders had not encountered a comb recently. Seeing her so, it was difficult to believe that this undernourished waif had been born to wealth and reared in luxury; squalor seemed her natural habitat. Yet Fletch had driven by her former home in Trousdale Estates, palatial even by the standards of the neighborhood which were as high as any in the city. He knew that she had been showered with every creature comfort money could buy; a Porsche was her sixteenth-birthday gift. He knew also that she had attended boarding school in Switzerland, was graduated from high school in Beverly Hills and studied for a year at UC-Santa Barbara where her major was philosophy. Timmy had been considered a model child by her teachers (by which teachers generally meant that she hadn't caused them any trouble) and something of a square by her contemporaries.

The seeds of her rebellion had undoubtedly been planted years earlier. It was college which caused them to flower. There she had fallen passionately in love—for the first time, apparently—and, as so often is the case, with the wrong man. Ken Lawton was a graduate student, a committed revolutionary and a friend of Lionel Gann. He helped organize the bloody riots at Isla Vista . . . and became their most noteworthy victim, killed by a stray police bullet. Her lover had set the insecure girl to questioning the values of the Establishment to which she belonged. His death caused her to declare war upon it. Here a concerned father might have made the difference but Ansel Towne was, as in the past, occupied with business and a new wife. He attempted to heal his daughter's trauma not with compassion but with a check. Timmy never cashed it. She cashed in her previous life instead. She left the university; from there her path led steadily downward, campus to commune and, eventually, to the cellars of the guerrilla underworld.

Following Sugarman's advice, Fletch felt no pity for her. Others had been dealt worse cards without being driven to tear up the deck. He himself had lost not only a mother but a father as well. He had been forced to con an indifferent world for a tiny fraction of what Timmy took as a matter of course. It was harder to obey Sugarman's second admonition, not to hate her. He accomplished this by viewing her as something other than a fellow human being. Rather, he considered her simply the key which would unlock the door behind which vengeance waited.

Before he could use the key, he must first possess it. He had still not hit upon the method by which this might be accomplished. The direct approach was the simplest yet Fletch doubted that it was the most productive. Timmy displayed a certain suspicion toward the men (always men, never women) she hustled. She accepted their money with childlike gratitude; she coldly rebuffed those who thought it might buy them more. The hackneyed boy-girl gambits, ranging from don't-I-know-you-from-someplace? to pardon-me-I-think-you-dropped-this, didn't seem likely to yield results, either.

He had nearly decided that the best course was to antagonize her by pretending to move in on her territory, counting on masculine charm to first placate, then ensnare her. Something happened which presented another alternative, no less a gamble but considerably more imaginative. An unmarked police sedan came cruising down the Alvarado Street hill, virtually crawling, to permit the plainclothesmen inside to scrutinize the park and its inhabitants.

Timmy saw them before they saw her. One moment she was facing the stream of pedestrian traffic in order to single out prospective contributors. The next moment she had submerged herself in it, becoming merely one more fish in a large school. Using the crowd as a protective screen, she found sanctuary in the nearby restroom. She did not emerge again for nearly twenty minutes—prudently, Fletch decided, since the police car made two more circles of the park before finally departing.

"Well, now," he murmured thoughtfully. Since begging

was a misdemeanor, Timmy had good reason to avoid the police—and, apparently, some experience in doing so. He could not logically pose as the friend of a friend . . . but the enemy of an enemy might be even better.

Timmy resumed her panhandling, seemingly confident that the danger was past. Promptly at five o'clock she quit, as she had on the previous day, her shift over. Fletch estimated that one out of four she solicited gave her something, perhaps a hundred all told. If the average gift was a quarter, Timmy had taken in close to twenty-five dollars, all profit and tax-free. Nor did she squander any of it on carfare; she crossed Wilshire Boulevard and held out her thumb until one of the passing motorists gave her a ride toward the downtown business district. COIN's investigators had been unable to discover where Lionel Gann's guerrilla cell was holed up. Fletch did not attempt to follow her. It was essential to his scheme that Timmy escort him there herself.

Sugarman had given him a number at which he could be reached, day or night; Fletch dialed it. "Where the hell have you been?" the general greeted him with a mixture of irritation and relief. "I expected to hear from you a week ago."

"I've been learning my lines, General."

Sugarman groaned. "You mean you still haven't made contact? What are you waiting for—an engraved invitation?"

"Something like that. I'm going to need your help to get it. Tell me, is there anyone in your organization who looks like a cop?"

"Are you serious, Orr? That's one of my problems. Most of my men look too damn much like cops."

"Good. Pick out the biggest and the meanest and have him at MacArthur Park tomorrow afternoon at four o'clock."

Sugarman demanded to know why; after Fletch explained, he grunted dubiously. "Sounds pretty risky to me. There must be an easier way." But, challenged to name it, he capitulated. "All right, it's your show. I'll send Hal Durham."

"He the toughest you've got?"

"We don't call him Bull just to be funny. He'll do the job for you. Anything else you need?"

"Yeah," Fletch told him. "Know any good prayers?"

He said one of his own that night. After that, there was nothing more to do except to wait for the following afternoon . . . and his answer. He reached MacArthur Park at three-thirty and found space for the Volkswagen a discreet distance removed from the beat Timmy patrolled. He was relieved to spy his quarry on her station. There had existed the possibility that she might decide to explore new territory elsewhere. Two of the principal characters in the impending drama were on hand. Fletch settled down to await the arrival of the third.

Bull Durham was not only on time, he was early. It still lacked five minutes of the hour when Fletch spotted him striding across the grass from the direction of the lake, a burly hard-faced man in a brown suit and matching fedora. His appearance—a shade too obviously the police officer to be the genuine article—left little doubt that this was indeed the COIN agent. What doubt remained was immediately dispelled by his actions. He knifed through the stream of pedestrians to seize Timmy by the arm. He held an open wallet briefly before the girl's startled eyes and then, following Fletch's scenario to the letter, thrust her toward the comparative seclusion of the lawn. A few of the passersby hesitated, staring curiously. A scowl and another flash of the wallet sent them on their way.

Fletch reached the pair in time to hear Timmy protest, "I don't know why you're arresting me. I wasn't doing anything wrong."

"What's going on?" Fletch inquired. "This guy bothering you?"

"Police officer," Durham told him briefly. "Buzz off, buddy."

"What's she done, anyway? I've been here all the time and—"

"Buzz off, I said. This isn't any of your business."

"She's got a right to know why you're busting her. That's the law."

"Look who's lecturing me on the law," Durham said ominously and Fletch hoped he wouldn't ruin everything by overacting. "Don't give me any lip, sonny, or I'll run you in too. Maybe I should, anyway. You're probably working this with her."

Timmy added her voice to his. "Please, fella, let it slide. I don't need any help. You'll only get yourself bent."

"Okay," Fletch agreed, shrugging. He winked at Durham to warn him what was coming and threw a roundhouse right at his jaw. Durham neither recognized the cue nor slipped the punch. It struck him squarely on the chin. He took two staggering steps backward and went down. He lay there, one leg twitching, glazed eyes staring at the sky.

The winner of the one-punch fight was nearly as stunned as the loser. He could not imagine how Durham, tipped off in advance, had allowed himself to be clobbered. But clobbered he was and Fletch could only hope that the blow had done no lasting damage. In any case, apologies must wait. Timmy, the reason for it all, was gaping at him incredulously. He grabbed her hand and dragged her toward the bus, ignoring her panted protests.

As the Volkswagen lurched away from the curb, he saw that a crowd was beginning to gather. Through their legs he glimpsed Durham on hands and knees, head tossing like a wounded moose. Good, the COIN agent wasn't seriously injured. In fact, Fletch suspected that he had come out the better of the two; his own hand felt as if he had broken it on the other man's jaw.

Worry relieved, he turned his attention to the woman. She huddled against the opposite door, regarding him with a wonderment she seemed unable to voice. "The word you're groping for is 'thanks,' " he told her.

"Thanks for what?" she retorted. "Why'd you ace in, anyway? Who needed you, tell me that?"

"I couldn't stand by and let the pig nick you."

"I've been nicked before. It's no big deal. All you have to do is play it cool, listen to the lecture, promise to be a good girl in the future, maybe cry a little—and then skip merrily on your way. You had to go and spoil it by coming on like Super Creep."

"Back that down the track a few feet, doll. Are you trying to say I blew it for you?"

"Man, are you ever quick! That's exactly what I'm saying. I had the best location in town. After what you did to Quinsler I can't go back there again ever. IQ's the type who never forgives or forgets."

"Quinsler?" Fletch repeated blankly.

"Sergeant Ike Quinsler, your favorite punching bag. We call him IQ because he doesn't have one. All he's got is a bad disposition and a good memory. He'll be playing the Inspector Javert bit with me for the rest of his life." She glared at him. "I don't see what's so funny about it!"

"Now that you mention it, neither do I." His laugh had been involuntary, born of shock not humor. In the recently concluded comedy, only he had been acting. The police officer, like the blow which felled him, had been all too genuine.

# Five

THE REAL HAL DURHAM, whoever he was, had made a trip for nothing . . . and Fletch had made an enemy. The damage was done and could not be retracted. He had no alternative except to forge ahead. "Okay," he said, regaining his composure, "what do we do now?"

"Unless you've got fleas, I don't know what you mean by 'we,'" Timmy snapped. "I didn't send for you and I'm not about to keep you. Just stop the car and let me out, will you?" She uttered a shriek as he applied the brakes. "Not in the middle of the street, dummy!" A chorus of horns echoed her exasperation. "I meant the sidewalk!"

Fletch obediently turned toward the curb. He did not stop upon reaching it but allowed the vehicle to bounce onto the sidewalk beyond, drawing another shriek from Timmy. "Now what's wrong? You said the sidewalk, didn't you!"

"No! I mean, yes—but you know darn well I didn't —" She gave up trying to sort sense from nonsense. "Will you please get back where you belong? What sort of a trip are you on, anyway?"

He found a more conventional parking place. "Did I finally get it right?" he asked hopefully.

Timmy stared at him with equal parts indignation and amusement. "You're absolutely bombed out of your skull," she declared finally. "You belong in a home."

"Right on. What's your address?"

34

"I didn't advertise for a roommate, thanks just the same."

"Don't knock it till you've tried it. I grow on people."

"So do warts." She opened the car door.

"Tell me something before you split. I just got into town from Berkeley. I need a pad to crash on. Any suggestions?"

"Try the yellow pages. Under 'M' for motels."

"No bread. Besides, the bims are looking for me. Under 'F' for fugitive."

Timmy raised her eyebrows. "That for real? What'd you do?"

"Let's put it this way. Certain of my activities at Cal caused me to depart that great university under a small cloud and in a big hurry. Does the name Chris Fletcher mean anything to you?" She shook her head. "Good, then maybe I've come far enough south. Or maybe you just aren't with it. Probably the latter."

"I get around," she replied with a touch of asperity. "And I'm a Cal gal myself. Santa Barbara."

"Oh, the country club of the south. Where we send the troops for R and R."

"Cool it, Mouth Man. We've done just as much fighting and bleeding and"—she swallowed hard and then finished in a choked voice—"and dying as you headline hounds up at Berkeley and don't you dare say we haven't!"

"Honey, when the history of the revolution is written, Santa Barbara will be only a footnote. You wouldn't even rate that if it hadn't been for Ken Lawton."

The name jolted her as he intended it should. "Did you know Ken?"

"I met him once or twice. We lost a damn good soldier there. And I'm not speaking for my fleas, either."

"I was his woman. I was with him when he—when he—"

35

"No lie? I didn't figure you for one of the brotherhood. You're too young."

"I'm old enough!" Timmy flared. "I've paid my dues —as much as you and maybe more."

"I wasn't trying to put you down, babe. Being young's no crime in my book. Neither is being pretty." He held up two fingers. "Peace."

The compliment mollified her somewhat. "No bones broken, I guess." As a further concession, she added, "They call me Timmy."

"Timmy," he repeated as though hearing it for the first time. "No good. I like 'honey' better. So will you, once you get used to it."

"That sounds like you expect to see me again."

"Is that too much to hope for?"

Timmy hesitated. "Yes," she said finally. "It might be fun but I'm not exactly a free agent. I'm sorry, really I am."

"Hell, don't go neurotic over it," he told her with feigned indifference. "I just thought that both of us being friends of Ken Lawton . . . Forget it. See you around."

Timmy did not accept her cue. The inference that she was in some fashion being unworthy of her dead lover caused her to squirm uneasily. "I said I was sorry," she muttered.

"And I said forget it." He allowed her to see that he was offended while inwardly he wondered if the tactic would be productive. His conman's instinct said yes, but he was not yet well enough acquainted with her to be certain.

His instinct was vindicated. She studied him, frowning, as if trying to reach a decision. At last she asked, "What are you going to do here in L.A.?"

"Oh, I don't know. Cruise around, look for more cops to slug."

"Seriously."

"Seriously, I still don't know. Submerge for a while, I

guess, wait for things to cool off so I can get back into action up north."

"If it's action you want, there's plenty right here. I might be able to plug you into something."

"I don't dig the panhandling scene, thanks."

"I mean heavy action," Timmy insisted. "Don't be so damn chauvinistic, Berkeley! Right now, this is where it's at."

"Lay it on me—in twenty-five words or less."

"Well, I belong to a little social betterment group. There could be an opening for the right man. I can't promise they'll buy you for the right man but I'll ask if you want me to."

Fletch did not leap at the offer. He did not wish to create suspicion by appearing too eager. "I'd have to look over the setup first. Who's your chairman?"

"Lionel Gann." She watched expectantly for his reaction and, receiving none, exclaimed, "Pappy Gann, for God's sake! He was Bruno Sledge's chief of staff."

"Sure he was. If I could have a meal for every nurd who claims he was big with Bruno, I'd never go hungry again."

"I'm just trying to cut you a huss," Timmy snapped. "So take it or shove it. I could care less."

"Good. I was afraid you might be getting emotionally involved." He grinned at her outraged gasp. "Okay, okay —I'll let you do me that favor. Take me to your leader."

East of the railroad yards lay the once-pleasant, now-squalid area known as Angel Heights. Ringed on all sides by freeways and begrimed by their fumes, it was an island of shabby homes and small stores and abandoned factories. The narrow streets were in need of rehabilitation and so too were many of those who lived on them. The city had made a start on both projects. A six-square-block area had been condemned and shortly would be cleared, with modern apartments replacing the ramshackle collection of multistory tenements and turn-of-the-century houses.

Whether this would dispel the aura of hopelessness that pressed down upon the slum neighborhood as tangibly as the smog—or whether, as opponents claimed, it would merely provide a better environment for the rats—was yet to be proved. The answer would not come soon in either case. The project (already dubbed Moran's Mistake in dubious homage to the city's mayor, who had conceived it) had run into litigation and out of money. Consequently the buildings languished like prisoners on death row, their future uncertain.

Timmy directed him to the end of one barricaded street. "You'll have to wait here. I don't dare take you any farther without Pappy's okay."

He watched her pry up a loose board in the fence and vanish behind it. So far, so good; he had won the first skirmish. He felt confident that Lionel Gann would not dismiss him without an audience. Simple curiosity could be counted on to gain him that much. And once he was within the enemy's camp . . . He could not anticipate the shape of the battle which lay ahead. He knew only that one or the other would not survive it.

The sun was setting when Timmy departed. Twilight arrived before she returned. "They hassled me some," she admitted. "But Pappy finally said bring you in so he can size you up. I had to argue like crazy to get that much, so walk soft, will you? For my sake?"

"What do you suggest I do—kiss his ring?"

"Just don't come on too strong about what a big man you are. I know that's asking an awful lot but give it a whirl, okay?"

"Yes, ma'am. Thank you very kindly, ma'am. That humble enough?"

"I'll bet you really crank it on at parties," she observed darkly.

He followed her through the fence. They entered an area which reminded Fletch of a studio back lot during the

38

slack season. The empty unlighted buildings gave the illusion of being merely façades and, rounding each corner, he halfway expected to encounter a cast and crew at work. But the street was deserted save for a rat sniffing through the debris. The rodent did not scamper away at their approach but surveyed them boldly. They not he were the trespassers here.

Their destination was a three-story apartment building whose gray stone walls, striped green by algae, caused to resembled a moldy loaf of bread stood on end. The date on the cornerstone proclaimed the loaf to be among the youngest of the derelicts; even so, it was twice Fletch's age. The doors were padlocked and the street-level windows boarded over. However, there was a fire escape in the alley, its rusty ladder reaching nearly to the pavement. Timmy led him up to the second floor, through a window from which the glass had been removed and into a dusty corridor. He could see little in the darkness but Timmy, taking him by the hand, padded confidently along the hall to the even greater darkness of the stairwell. He expected to climb higher. They descended instead, past the ground floor and into the basement beneath.

Here the light was better but the air was worse and both for the same reason: a score of candles placed strategically about the concrete cavern. Their smoke mingled with the aroma of boiled cabbage and the fumes from the kerosene cook stove, creating an atmosphere which assaulted the eyes as well as the nostrils. The furniture (if it could be dignified as such) consisted of wooden boxes of various sizes, the bench seat from an automobile, a galvanized washtub with scrub board, a refrigerator whose door had been removed and which held, not food, but ammunition and explosives—and a portable television set. Yet the basement was surprisingly tidy for all its Early Garage Sale décor. The floor had been swept, and recently; the sleeping bags were rolled up and stacked neatly in a corner.

All this Fletch took in at a glance. He stood among his brother's murderers; he fixed his gaze upon their faces, studying each in turn to fix them forever in his memory. The cellar's occupants numbered six in all, four males and two females. None was over thirty and most were considerably short of that age. Their hair was long and their clothing nondescript—and sexless inasmuch as the costumes could have been interchangeable. They sat cross-legged on the floor or perched upon the wooden boxes and returned his scrutiny with the curiosity of a jury inspecting the accused.

"Well, here he is," Timmy announced unnecessarily. "Meet Chris Fletcher."

No one spoke. The group seemed to be waiting for permission; Fletch smiled at the one who would give it. He needed no introduction to recognize Lionel Gann, called Pappy. Neither his bearing nor his apparel identified him as the leader. He was, in fact, the smallest of the males, slender as a girl with delicate hands and an ascetic hollow-cheeked face framed with black hair like a cameo and dominated by deep-set smoldering eyes. The others were still children, whatever their chronological age. Lionel Gann was a man, and a sophisticated one.

He continued his inspection of the newcomer as if he could, through sheer will, see past flesh to the soul beneath. Fletch recognized it as a device to put him on the defensive. He terminated the silence by declaring loudly, "Succotash!"

Gann's satanic eyebrows rose and his disciples shifted their positions, the spell broken. "What is that supposed to convey?"

"I figured you were waiting for me to give the password."

Timmy said nervously, "I warned you he's some kind of joker."

"Is that what he is?" Gann cupped his bearded chin in

his palm while keeping his eyes fixed on Fletch's face. "Timmy's told us how you convinced her to bring you here. We'd appreciate hearing why."

"Mind if I sit down?" He did so without waiting for permission, thereby making himself more their guest than their adversary. "Now let's take it again from the top. I didn't convince Timmy, she convinced me. She thought maybe we could work something out."

"Really? What exactly do you have to offer?"

Fletch shrugged. "Bench strength. I know the game— and I play all positions."

"I'm not sure I understand. What game do you mean?"

"Screw the System, ever hear of it? Or have I stumbled into a meeting of the Angel Heights Rotary by mistake?"

A couple of the group smiled; Gann did not. "If I read you correctly, you're asking to join us. We're very flattered, naturally. But forgive us if we're just a wee bit suspicious, too. Anybody can grow a beard and shout 'screw the system'—even a pig. Could be that's what you are, a narc or a fed or another one of General Sugarman's storm troopers."

"Hey, you're some kind of joker yourself, aren't you? But in case that crap is for real, hear this loud and clear. I don't know you any more than you know me and it won't break my heart to keep it that way. All I did was try to keep your bunny from being nicked—and all I've gotten for it is the shaft, first from her, now from you. Who the hell needs it, anyway?"

"I didn't say you were a pig," Gann replied, unruffled by the outburst. "I said you could be. Just like you could have staged the thump with IQ so you could penetrate this tribe."

"Man, you're simply too much! I broke my hand and maybe his jaw just to hype you? What for—so I could bust you for littering? That's about all you're capable of, or I miss my guess."

"Being snotty buys you nothing, Fletcher. Remember, we didn't invite you here."

"Timmy did."

"Timmy has a lot to learn." Gann turned his dark gaze momentarily in her direction; she winced. "But the damage—or whatever—is already done. If you're what you claim to be, beautiful. But if you're not . . ." He left the threat dangling.

After a moment, Fletch spread his hands in a sheepish gesture. "So I got a little bent. I'm not used to being chopped by the brotherhood." He met Gann's probing eyes solemnly. "I swear that I am not now, nor have I ever been, a narc or a fed. The only general I know is general delivery. I am, or was, tactical operations officer, Student Revolutionary Council, Berkeley. You can check me out with them."

"That won't be necessary. We've got a former member of the SRC right here." Gann turned to the blond girl who sat cross-legged beside him. "You've looked and listened, Blossom. He doesn't seem to recognize you—but do you recognize him?"

# Six

FLETCH HAD WEIGHED the possibility of encountering someone able to brand him a fraud and had discounted it on the
basis of the odds. His stomach contracted as he realized that
he had lost the gamble—and with it, possibly, his life.
Two alternatives were open to him. He could run or he
could attempt to brazen it out. The first might save his
skin but it would terminate his mission, robbing him of the
vengeance he sought. He chose the second. Outwardly
calm, he waited for the inevitable denunciation while his
mind searched feverishly for the argument which would
blunt it.

"Speak up," Gann prompted. "Do you know him or
don't you?"

The girl called Blossom flushed, appearing not to relish
her judicial role. She was among the youngest of the
group, delicate in build, with the expression of an eager-
to-please puppy and hair that flowed down her back like a
mantle of corn silk. She cleared her throat. Then, to
Fletch's astonishment, she said in a voice barely above a
whisper, "Sure, Pappy—sure, I know him."

"Then why didn't you say so in the beginning?"

"You said let you do the talking," Blossom replied with
a child's plaintive logic. She gave Fletch an ingratiating
smile. "I guess you don't remember me. I'm Blossom—
Huey O'Haver's assistant? I used to sit in for him at
Council sometimes."

"If you say so," Fletch agreed, avoiding the temptation to overplay his hand with a too-quick acknowledgment. "Huey had his people and I had mine. I never paid that much attention to the other sections. Seems to me I've seen you around, though. How you been, Blossom?"

"Smokey, thanks," she said gratefully, as if she rather than he had been vindicated. "What's shaking at Berkeley, anyway? I've been out of touch since I came south. Is Huey still raising hell?"

"Do you need to ask, knowing Huey?"

"God, no! Do you remember the time when—"

"You two can go head on later," Gann interrupted. "It seems that you're out front, after all, Fletcher. Sorry if I gave you a rough time. We can't afford to take chances." He extended a hand. "Welcome to the PTA."

"Pappy's Tiny Army?"

That produced a chuckle all around. "Appropriate but inaccurate. No, PTA stands for Parent Teacher Association, just like that other group, but without the hyphen. We're parent teachers. We aim to instruct their generation in a new and better way of life."

"I'm for that. What's your curriculum?"

"Nothing terribly structured. We're just hanging loose, preparing ourselves for our mission—mentally, spiritually and financially." Gann shook his head reproachfully. "I really can't thank you for clobbering IQ, no matter how good your intentions were. We need the bread that Timmy was bringing in. You've put her out of work, at least for the present."

"Look on the bright side. You've gained another pair of willing hands."

"Let me clarify your status, Fletcher. Timmy offered you a pad to crash on—temporarily—and I'll honor her promise. But as for you joining us . . . Well, we're a tight-knit tribe, small because that's the way we want it. The vibrations are good. I'm not sure you'd fit in. I'd have

44

to know you better before I could say. You're welcome to stick around for a day or so on that basis if you'd like."

Fletch accepted the grudging hospitality with thanks. Gann introduced him to the other members of the PTA. Most were identified only by first names, or nicknames, as if thereby to sever any connection with their former families. Rufus Wren was the exception. He retained his patronym, perhaps because it fit him so well. There was something birdlike about him in the way he cocked his red-tufted head and in his chirping speech; he appeared to perch instead of sit, to hop rather than walk. The other men were Choogle and Injun. The third woman was Midge, a stocky unsmiling creature who wore no bra beneath her T-shirt and needed none, one-of-the-boys in all save anatomy. Choogle was tall and gangling, with bad teeth and a worse complexion, passionate in his convictions but too shy to be able to articulate them, the type referred to in the Marxist lexicon as "the useful idiot." In any lexicon, there was only one term which described the bare-chested Injun and that was "savage." His broad flat face with its high cheekbones and thin nose did make him resemble an Apache brave, although he hailed from Arkansas, not Arizona. The resemblance was further enhanced by a beaded headband which bound his coarse black hair and by the bone-handled scalping knife thrust in his belt. The others welcomed Fletch with varying degrees of cordiality. Injun's greeting was a cold stare and a slight nod.

"We're going to have to do something about your car," Gann decided. "The pigs may have gotten the license number. Rufus, see if you can't find a place to hide it."

"It's almost time for the Early Show," Rufus Wren protested. "Vintage Bogart and you know how I—" His eyes encountered Gann's and he rose with a sigh. "Forgive me, Bogey."

Fletch rose too. "I'd better go with you. I need my sleeping bag and my teddy bear. Save me some chow, okay? My jaws are really tight."

"You've got a shock coming," Wren muttered as he led Fletch back up the stairs. "Chasen's this ain't. Ever had Peasant's Porridge?"

"Is that the recipe that begins: First, skin one peasant . . . ?"

Wren giggled. "We should be so lucky. The only fresh meat we get around here is when Injun traps a rat. We're very large on carrot tops and mustard greens, though. And corn meal! We have it baked, fried, boiled and steamed, every way except on the rocks. God, am I ever sick of corn meal!"

"Sounds to me like you should fire the chef."

"Wouldn't help. Pappy doesn't believe in squandering our money on food." He added quickly, "He's right, too. We got more important things to do with it. That's one of the rules. Everything goes into the kitty for later on. Welcome to the poorhouse, Fletcher. I used to listen to my old man spouting off about the Great Depression. Hell, he didn't know what hard times were!"

"Well, he did have to get along without a TV."

"Already it starts." Wren sighed. "Lay off, will you? I swallow enough of that from the others. So maybe we could get twenty-five bucks for the box—but how'd we know what's going on if we couldn't watch the news? And since Pappy agrees that we gotta know what's going on, where's the harm in me sneaking in a movie now and then? I happen to be an aficionado of the cinema."

"I'm into that myself. In some circles, I'm worshipped as an authority."

"Not here, you ain't. When it comes to films, I yield to no man. I'm writing the complete and unexpurgated history of the movies. In nine and a half volumes."

"Why nine and a half?"

"Why not?" Wren replied logically. "So you pose as an expert, huh? We'll see about that. Who played the title role in *Frankenstein?*"

"Colin Clive. You didn't really think I was going to say Karloff, did you? Coming back at you—in what movie did Gary Cooper keep falling off his horse?"

"*Alice in Wonderland.* Same flick, who played Alice?"

"Charlotte Henry, natch."

"Outasight!" Wren exclaimed. "Hey, I'm gonna enjoy having you around."

"If I decide to stick. Pappy's rules may not be my rules."

"Oh, they're not all that bad. No personal property, nobody owns anything—I already mentioned that. Otherwise, well . . . No liquor or drugs. Pot's okay but acid's a no-no. Ditto speed, uppers and downers, and all the hard stuff." He broke into a chant, "We're the kids from the PTA, pure as snow in every way."

"How about sex?"

"How about that! Yeah, we got a rule there too. If you've got an itch and can find somebody to scratch it, feel free. But it's gotta be mutual. Also temporary."

"No pairing off, you mean."

"We're supposed to be free spirits here. Emphasis on 'supposed.' I mean, Blossom's got a thing for Pappy, poor child. Choogle nurses a peculiar attraction for Midge while she has eyes only for Injun. Thus doth Mother Nature foul up the detail."

"Who does that leave you—Timmy?"

"Would you hate me if I said yes?" Wren asked shrewdly. "Needn't fret, chum. I'm homosexual. Does that bother you?"

"Not unless you do."

"Oh, it's largely latent. I sublimate here and compensate elsewhere. So if you've got your radar locked onto the fair Timmy, I figure Injun is your only real competition. There is one horny Huron."

"Solid. When did the Indians ever win?"

"Ask Custer. Injun may only fantasize the redskin bit but he's a for-real primitive. You see that knife he carries? He knows how to use it—if you care to believe what it says on his dishonorable discharge."

"Please, let's show a little respect for our gallant fighting men."

"My point exactly. There's no way you're going to make a friend out of Injun because that's against his religion. Just try to fix it so he doesn't hate you more than the rest of the world." Wren dropped his bantering tone for a rare moment of somber reflection. "Beats me why Pappy keeps him around. He's not really one of us and never will be."

Fletch, more knowledgeable regarding human nature than he, could surmise the reason. Like any seeker of power, Lionel Gann needed his hatchet man, the indispensable muscle behind the message. Every revolution, large or small, had its Injun to do the dirty work and, usually, to be dispensed with later when his talents were no longer required. Occasionally the hatchet man was the one who did the dispensing—witness Stalin—and that was a danger that Gann must be well aware of. So, rather than fearing Injun, Fletch welcomed his presence as a possible weapon to use against his master.

As a beginning, he said, "Yeah, I've known others like him. You never can be sure what side they're really on."

"I'm not capping on Injun, understand," Wren replied, a shade defensively. "His thing is not my thing but, what the hell, in diversity there is strength, right?"

Fletch did not pursue the subject. Rufus Wren had already disclosed that a division existed within the PTA. It would be foolish for him to choose sides; better that he stand aloof and attempt to pit one against the other.

A gate had been placed in the fence which surrounded the instant ghost town to permit demolition equipment to enter and exit. Wren, who seemed as familiar with the area as the rats, opened the padlock with a crude pick and waved the bus through, securing the gate behind it.

"This is probably safe enough," he judged. "But since Pappy said hide it, let's give it the full treatment."

The concealment he had in mind was a former grocery store from which the rear wall had already been removed. Fletch learned that it had been the PTA's original home. They had occupied the condemned buildings for nearly a year, moving from one to the next a step ahead of the wrecking crews. "We lived high on the hog at first," Wren bragged. "People left food and all sorts of junk behind. We even had electricity for a while. Now all we got left is the water. When that goes, we do too, I guess."

Exactly where, Wren didn't know. Nor did he appear to have any clear understanding of what the cell's mission amounted to. "They'll tell us when the time comes." They? The Co-op, the politburo of the urban guerrilla coalition to which Lionel Gann belonged and which ruled the terrorist movement with an iron hand. It bothered Wren not in the slightest that the organization whose watchwords were peace, freedom and equality practiced none of them.

During the remainder of the evening, he had the opportunity to study the other members of the PTA. They and he belonged to the same generation, children of the atom, the computer and the cathode ray tube, weaned on Spock, nourished by Disney and the Beatles, with a sophistication learned as much from *Mad Magazine* as from McLuhan. He like they had been inspired by Camelot, appalled by assassination and puzzled by the spectacle of man simultaneously reaching for the stars while groveling in the slime. Yet try as he might, Fletch could not identify with his companions. At some point they had departed the mainstream and, with it, the vast majority of their peers. The guerrillas believed themselves to be the architects of a new social justice; he saw them as the advocates of an old bar-

barism.

On the surface, they seemed unlikely material from which to mold nihilistic revolutionaries. With the exception of Injun, they were above average in intelligence, better educated than most including Fletch and, he guessed, the product of well-to-do, even wealthy, homes. Yet each had deliberately defected from his society and it was unfair to cast Gann as their Svengali. He had merely guided them in structuring a substitute. Choice not coercion held them here. Reacting from permissiveness, they had embraced a rigid discipline. Rejecting luxury, they had chosen squalor. Fletch was struck by the irony of it. While congratulating themselves on spurning "the rat race," they had turned themselves quite literally into rats, living off refuse and hunted like vermin.

Yet rats could kill . . . and he wondered which one of them had placed his brother's drugged body in the path of the onrushing train. The surly Injun? Choogle? Gann himself? Was Rufus Wren's high-pitched giggle the last sound Curt had heard? Or had his final conscious sight been of a softer, more attractive face? Not that it mattered; the guilt was indivisible and large enough for all to share.

Following supper (boiled okra and corn meal cakes, which proved as unpalatable as Wren had predicted), Gann summoned them together for a rap session. It turned out to be an inquisition with Timmy in the dock. The newest apostle was prodded by the others, often cruelly, to confess past heresies and recant false gods. No subject was taboo. Her values were mocked, her motives impugned; she was accused of sins that ranged from materialism to masturbation. Fletch guessed that this was not the first such interrogation she had been subjected to. Nor would it be the last. After an hour, Gann dismissed the now-sobbing girl with "That'll do for tonight."

Reprieved but not absolved, Timmy crept away to her sleeping bag, the picture of exhaustion. The rest drifted off

50

also, Wren to the television set where Choogle and the women joined him, Injun to some errand upstairs. Fletch was left alone with the soft-voiced leader.

"Care to critique the performance?" Gann inquired, one professional to another.

"The lack of thumbscrews was scarcely noticed. Are you that rough on everyone?"

"Timmy's a special case. You might compare her to a bottle that's contained poison. She's got to be rinsed out thoroughly before she can be used."

"She seems pretty well rinsed to me."

"The fact that she brought you here—against orders —proves otherwise. She still hasn't gotten rid of her bourgeois passion for Ken Lawton. All you had to do was invoke his name and"—Gann snapped his fingers— "she forgot everything I've tried to teach her."

"She's just a kid—and kids make mistakes."

"I can't accept that. Group security demands total loyalty to the group. Anything less can be fatal. Suppose you'd turned out to be an enemy agent?"

"Luckily, I didn't."

"Yes," Gann agreed softly. "Luckily for you—and for Timmy."

"Level with me, Pappy. All this talk about enemy agents penetrating the tribe—is that just to impress the troops or has it actually happened?"

He waited for Gann to condemn himself out of his own mouth. Gann gave him an enigmatic smile instead. "What I'm saying is that we have to be on our guard, all of us, all the time. Against everyone—including ourselves."

"But if we can't trust each other, who can we trust?"

"No one. To trust is to perish. You've read Marighella on the subject, naturally."

"Naturally," Fletch lied. He knew that the slain Latin American terrorist was revered by the urban guerrillas only slightly less than Mao and considerably more than

Che but that was the extent of his knowledge. He dared not confess his ignorance; Gann would have thought it strange. To head off a possible interrogation on the subject, he added, "It's been a while, though."

"Take a refresher course," Gann suggested, tossing him a sheaf of mimeographed papers fastened together with staples. "Just be sure to give it back before you leave. It's the only copy we have."

Fletch accepted the loan with a nod of thanks. The words which accompanied it confirmed his suspicion that Gann was not eager to have him join the PTA. Gann recognized the newcomer as more a leader than a follower and there was room for only one leader. Fletch's task was to convince him that he had no designs on the crown while at the same time making himself appear a valuable recruit. It called for a delicate blend of deference and arrogance. He must bow his head without bending his back, thus becoming that most prized of all lieutenants, the one able to initiate as well as obey, Stonewall Jackson to Gann's Lee. Or more accurately, considering his intentions, Iago to Gann's Othello.

For the moment, however, he was still the outsider. Gann, considering the conversation concluded, joined the others to watch the late evening newscast. He did not invite Fletch to do likewise or to share the homemade joints he passed around. Fletch edged closer, anyway, and Wren, the most congenial of the group, obligingly made room for him in the circle. "There's a real classic on the Late Show tonight," Wren informed him. "The original *Dracula* with Lugosi and—"

"Hush up," Gann ordered. "I want to hear this."

"This" was the daily wrapup on the Bruno Sledge trial, now in its eighth month and presumably nearing its conclusion since the defense had called its final witnesses. The reporter's commentary, interspersed with film clips and an artist's drawings of the accused and his attorney, drew obscene comments from the tiny audience. The women were especially vehement in denouncing the Establishment— "Toppies" in their jargon—and in accusing its lackeys, the news media, of flagrant bias. Called on to share their indignation, Fletch startled them by refusing.

"Hey, man!" Midge cried angrily. "Whose team you on, anyway?"

Fletch sighed. "Are you really that lame? Sure, the whole scene is a bummer. Bruno was convicted before it ever began. What the Toppies don't realize is that they're on trial too. The stronger they come on with their stacked deck, the better for us. They're proving what we've been preaching all along, that their so-called justice is just a cover for political repression."

"You mean it doesn't tick you off that Bruno isn't getting a fair trial?"

"You've got to take the long view, child. A revolution needs its martyrs. Where would Christianity be today if the Sanhedrin had given Jesus a fair trial?" He turned toward Gann. "You're the resident guru, Pappy. Am I right or wrong?"

Few men can resist the flattery of being appealed to for judgment. Gann, though reluctant to side with the stranger, succumbed to it. "He's right, Midge. Partly, anyhow. That circus they're holding at the courthouse is bound to make a lot of fence-sitters wonder if Bruno is being tried for what he did or for what he believes. We can exploit that. On the other hand, I think it's a little too soon to write Bruno off as a martyr." He gave Fletch an enigmatic smile. "Unless our visiting lecturer knows something I don't."

Fletch smiled back. "I don't even know enough to keep my mouth shut. I was just rapping for the fun of it. I didn't mean to put anybody down."

Yet the argument—and Gann's grudging endorsement—had served to make him less of an alien.

Midge guessed that she saw what he was getting at, all right, "now that Pappy's explained it." Rufus Wren gave him a friendly wink and one of the marijuana cigarettes. Fletch, like most of his peer group, had tried the narcotic and, again like most, had found little benefit in it. He considered pot no more immoral than alcohol. He eschewed both as crutches he didn't need. He accepted Wren's offer now because his companions would have viewed a refusal as suspicious. He inhaled the sweetish smoke leisurely, pronounced it good and was affected by it not at all.

For the others, the act seemed to verge on the sacramental. They puffed silently and solemnly, their expressions rapt, as if contemplating or expecting to contemplate some profound mystery. After a while, Blossom began to strum softly on the guitar she was rarely without and then to sing in a small true voice, a melancholy ballad which spoke wistfully of love and peace and universal brotherhood. Tears trickled down her cheeks as she sang. When she had finished, several of her audience murmured, "All right!" like an amen.

The song served as taps for the evening. Midge unrolled her sleeping bag outside the radius of the candle glow, stripped without embarrassment and went to sleep. Rufus Wren and Choogle lugged the television to a far corner of the cellar in order to watch the late night movie without disturbing the others. Fletch declined the invitation to join them, pleading fatigue. He spread his own sleeping bag a short distance from where Timmy slumbered, only the top of her head visible in the quilted cocoon.

Gann remained where he was, sitting cross-legged and staring at nothing, a brooding prophet communing with his god. For a time Blossom kept the silent vigil with him, her eyes fixed doglike upon her master's face, awaiting his pleasure. Finally, she put a tentative hand on his knee to remind him of her presence. Gann brushed it off impatiently and the girl, chastened, crept away. But the spell was broken. Gann stretched and yawned, then relit his half-smoked joint from the remaining candle before extinguishing it, leaving the television the only illumination. Shortly afterward, Injun returned to the cellar. Fletch became aware of his presence only because Injun was forced to step over him to reach his objective. He squatted beside Timmy and began to prod the sleeping girl and to whisper softly in her ear. Timmy's reply was to snuggle deeper inside the bag until not even the top of her blond head was visible. Injun scowled. With a glance around, he seized the bag's zipper release. His gaze encountered Fletch's. For a moment their eyes locked, then Injun rose with a shrug of his bare muscular shoulders. He crossed the cellar to where Midge slept. There he was welcome. Midge sat up, a white shadow in the gloom that was shortly obscured by the man's darker one. Their lovemaking was swift and violent. Sated, Injun rolled onto his back and almost immediately began to snore.

The public coupling did not surprise Fletch. It was a common practice in every primitive society and the PTA, for all its sophisticated rhetoric, was just that. He was intrigued by the fact that Timmy had refused to indulge in it. This seemed to confirm Gann's accusation that she had not yet wholly embraced the guerrilla ethic. Heretofore, he had seen the girl as an unwitting accomplice useful only in gaining entree to the enemy. For the first time he began to picture her as a potential weapon, equally unwitting, with which he might destroy them. If Timmy's primary allegiance still belonged to her dead lover rather than her new comrades—and if he could induce her to transfer that allegiance to himself . . . Other revolutions had perished through betrayal from within its own ranks. It was an avenue worth exploring. For the moment, however, he was too fatigued to take more than the first step. He drifted off to sleep among his foes with the still-glowing television screen as a comforting night light.

When he awoke sometime later the television was dark but it was not yet morning. Something had touched his face. His first horrified reaction was that it had been a rat. But a rat did not have fingers, nor was even the most educated of rodents able to operate the zipper of a sleeping bag. The presence was human and, he discovered as their bodies made contact, female. There could be no doubt about that: the woman who had joined him in his bed was nude.

"Timmy?" he asked—with some difficulty since her palm was pressed against his mouth. Did she think he was going to scream? he wondered.

"It's me," she whispered and he realized that his visitor was Blossom. That settled the question of who but not why. "I'm sorry I woke you up, Fletch. I had to talk to you."

"Sure," he said, removing her hand from his mouth. "But is it okay if I breathe?"

"I was afraid you might holler. I didn't want anybody to hear me. Fletch, I came to tell you how grateful I am for what you did."

"Yeah?" he replied, thankful that the darkness concealed his bewilderment. What was she talking about, anyway?

"God, was I scared!" Blossom went on. "You showing up here, a big wheel from Berkeley—the real twenty-four-karat item, what I've only been pretending to be—and I had to sit there, waiting for you to pull the covers off me. I knew you didn't know me. I mean, how could you? I was just a nobody up there, a zero, zilch. I never really worked with Huey O'Haver, he doesn't know I'm alive. And then when you said that maybe you did remember me . . . You saved my ass, no kidding!"

"Ain't no big thing," Fletch assured her. So that mystery was solved: Blossom had not exposed him for fear that she herself would be exposed, unaware that his lie was even greater than hers. "Why the act, though? So you weren't large at Berkeley—what the hell does it matter here?"

"I wanted Pappy to think I was somebody. Not just a mental hernia, the way it's always been. So I scabbed a little and then a little bit more and pretty soon I was in too deep to back out."

"You're pretty flipped over him, aren't you?"

"Yeah, I guess so. It's against the rules—but I can't help it." She added bravely, "I think he grooves on me too, at least a little. And maybe someday we'll—" She stopped, unwilling to admit that her dream of the future was not so different, after all, from those she professed to scorn.

Fletch felt pity for her since he doubted that Lionel Gann's future—if, indeed, he had one—would include her except peripherally. Gann was married to revolution; he needed no other mate. "Hang in there, baby. And don't worry about me. I won't cut the rope."

"You're beautiful," she told him. "Well, I guess I'd better creep back to my own crib. I mean, unless you'd like me to . . ."

He could not deny that her naked flesh aroused desire in him. The temptation to think only of the moment was strong but he overcame it. It would be a mistake for him, the stranger, to take one of the tribe's women—and the leader's woman, at that—even with her consent. Furthermore, as matters stood, Blossom was in his debt. It might be prudent to leave the account unsettled, a hedge against misfortune. So he said, "Hey, you just got through telling me your heart belongs to Pappy. I appreciate the offer of the rest but wouldn't you really prefer that we just stay good friends?"

She gave him a chaste and sisterly kiss, a conclusion rather than a beginning. "Gee, I'm glad you're here! You're real people, Fletch."

So that was his reward, her gratitude instead of her body. It remained to be seen if he had made a good bargain.

# Seven

ONE WALL OF THE CELLAR was devoted to graffiti, a collection of witticisms and aphorisms to which all the members of the PTA contributed as the spirit moved them. They ranged from the political ("Patriotism is murder set to march music") to the theological ("God does not celebrate Thanksgiving") and the classical ("When Jason divorced Medea, she got the children"). Some were insults directed at Establishment leaders: "Otis Moran isn't worth a farthing, much less a belching." Others were sex-based vulgarisms: "Story of two happy fags—Morris Fitzpatrick and Patrick Fitzmorris."

A few were even in verse and at this art form Timmy was the acknowledged master. Fletch watched as she added her latest effort:

> I have a favorite joke.
> Have you a favorite, too?
> Mine is me—
> Is yours you?

His compliments embarrassed her. "I was always hung on poetry, but Emily Dickinson's got no cause to worry. Here—you take a crack at it."

He declined on the grounds that he was not yet one of the tribe. "Who knows? I may get me a wall of my own and go into business for myself."

Breakfast consisted of more corn meal, steamed as a cereal, studded with dried apricots and drenched with powdered milk, all products with which the PTA was amply supplied, courtesy of the state's food subsidy program. The women took turns at preparing the meals and cleaning up afterward. The men stood aloof from these and other housekeeping tasks. Lionel Gann didn't even bother to roll up his own sleeping bag; Blossom gladly assumed that responsibility for him. Fletch was amused to note that the rebels practiced the same sort of discrimination against which they inveighed, not only sexually but racially. They spoke earnestly of "our black/brown/red brothers" while at the same time maintaining a closed circle which was exclusively Caucasian.

Following breakfast, the guerrillas prepared to sally forth into what they referred to as "the people farm." With the exception of their leader, each was profitably employed. Blossom and Midge were flower children in more than name; they operated a sidewalk stand with merchandise culled from the discards of the city's wholesale flower market. Choogle worked in a car wash. Rufus Wren had found a vocation worthy of his facile mind and prodigious memory, supplying ghost-written term papers to students at the city's two major universities. Injun was a floater with no steady job; he picked up a few dollars, legally or otherwise, as the opportunity presented itself. Only Gann was exempt from earning a living. He, Fletch gathered, was too occupied with strategy to be bothered with such mundane matters.

The question arose as to a new assignment for Timmy since returning to MacArthur Park was temporarily, and perhaps permanently, impossible. Nor, with Sergeant Quinsler seeking vengeance, did it seem advisable to resume her begging at a new location.

Gann decided that she should try her luck at shoplifting instead. "Hit some of the downtown department stores. IQ won't be looking for you there and maybe you can rip off something we can pawn."

"Gee, I don't know," Timmy murmured, obviously not relishing the new role. "I never did anything like that before."

Fletch seized his opportunity. "Hey, why don't I go along and teach you the skinny? That is, unless Pappy has some objection."

Gann hesitated. "No objection," he said finally. "It could help Timmy to have somebody riding shotgun. And I guess you might as well earn your keep—as long as you're here."

Fletch ignored the innuendo and drew Timmy aside. "Just hold on to Daddy's hand and he'll get you through safely."

She took his advice literally, giving his fingers a thankful squeeze. "It's real tall, you going with me. I don't think I could hack it alone."

"Anyone can steal. The trick is not to get caught. That's my function. Do you have a decent dress and a pair of heels? Solid. Bring them along and you can change in the car. Oh, and we'll have to do something about your hair, too. Like, comb it."

He explained his reasoning on their way to the Volkswagen's makeshift garage. "It's a matter of image. Statistics prove that nine out of ten shoplifters are women, mostly young women between the ages of fifteen and twenty-five. So you're automatically a suspicious character to the store protection people. And if you sashay in dressed like one of those hippie commie freaks besides, you might as well wear a sign saying Watch Me! You'd be lucky to get away with a paper towel from the ladies' room. Our first job is to transform you into a reasonable facsimile of an American girl."

"Don't make it sound so hard," she replied, a trifle nettled. "I may know from nothing about shoplifting but I've had a lot of practice being a girl. I've even been told I do it

60

pretty well."

"Talk's cheap," he scoffed. Yet when she emerged from the camper fifteen minutes later he gave a low-pitched whistle of approval. Gone was the street urchin. In her place stood a handsome young woman, smartly attired in a demure blue frock ruffled at throat and wrists in frothy white. Her legs were sheathed in nylon, her feet were shod in leather. Timmy had tied her blond hair into a ponytail and added a touch of color to her lips and cheeks and eyes.

"You like?" she asked hopefully.

"I like. Only trouble is, everybody's going to ask, 'What's a bitchen bunny like her doing with a crud like him?' Pardon me while I use the dressing room."

He discarded his shabby costume for suit and tie. His transformation was not as startling as hers since it did not include his face. However, beards were acceptable nearly everywhere these days and his had not yet reached the stage of appearing unkempt. "That makes it, I guess," he judged. "Amerika, may I present—Mr. and Mrs. Straight Arrow!"

Timmy laughed with a trace of wistfulness. "I wouldn't admit it to anyone but you—but it feels kinda nice to wear something pretty for a change."

"Watch your tongue, girl. I might report you."

"You won't. I don't know how I know that but I do. I feel, well, like we swing from the same tree."

"How about the other monkeys?"

"Same forest, different trees." She added quickly, "I'm not putting anybody down, though. I mean, if I don't always relate to them, that's my hangup, right?"

"Maybe." He was tempted to encourage her to believe otherwise but his conman's instinct cautioned against moving too rapidly. "One thing I do know. If we don't get this show on the road, Pappy'll put me down."

Gann had suggested that they make the downtown department stores their target. Fletch drove out Wilshire

Boulevard to Beverly Hills instead. He had two reasons for disobeying instructions. He revealed one of them to Timmy. "The pickings should be better. We don't want to mess with nickel-and-dime junk." The other reason, which he kept to himself, was that the scheme he had concocted required that Timmy's victims be well acquainted with the name of Towne.

"We split up here," he told her as they neared the entrance to the community's largest and most exclusive store. "I'll be nearby in case of trouble but you're on your own from now on. Remember everything I taught you?"

"I wander around for a while to see what can be picked up from the counters. Then I buy something inexpensive and ask for a shopping bag to put it in. I use the bag to carry the loot—"

"Stick to small items. Watches, jewelry, cameras, field glasses, electric shavers, wallets, transistor radios—there's always a market for that stuff. Lay off the clothing and the cosmetics. They're worthless." He studied her appraisingly. "Just one more thing. Stop shaking!"

"I'm scared spitless," she admitted.

"Nobody's asking you to spit." He gave her a parting pat of comfort. "I promised to take care of you. Have faith."

He watched her march into the store, shoulders squared bravely as if on her way to the gallows. After a moment, he followed. He hovered a discreet distance away while Timmy tried on hats and fingered dresses. Occasionally he glanced at the clock and scowled, the annoyed husband waiting for his wife to appear. When Timmy at last made her purchase, a scarf, he sought out the service desk and asked to be directed to the store's security detail.

The store detective, informed of the request by telephone, came to meet him instead. He was a middle-aged man named Waters, a former police officer ideally suited to his job in that his plump body and cherubic face did not suggest "cop" in the slightest. His greeting was not a growled "What seems to be the trouble?" but a suave "May I be of service to you?"

Fletch introduced himself and indicated Timmy who, two aisles removed, was hovering near a display of cameras. "See that girl over there, the one in the blue dress? I want to warn you that she's about to boost some goods."

"That so?" Waters said, his eyes narrowing. Then they widened with skepticism. "Did you say 'about to'? How can you possibly know—"

"Trust me," Fletch begged. As if responding to a cue, Timmy, after a covert glance around, slipped one of the cameras into her shopping bag. The theft accomplished, she scurried away, so obviously guilty that her instructor winced.

"Well, well," Waters murmured. "I still don't understand how you knew but you certainly did. Much obliged, Mr. Fletcher. I guess I'd better have a little chat with the young lady."

"I'd appreciate it if you didn't. So would her father. That's Timothea Towne—Ansel Towne's daughter."

Waters clucked his tongue. "I thought she looked familiar. The Townes are among our best customers. Why on earth would she . . ." He shook his head in bewilderment, then said self-righteously, "I guess it doesn't matter. Stealing is stealing, no matter who does it."

"Timmy is a very sick girl," Fletch informed him. "She's under a psychiatrist's care. She probably should be confined but you know how fathers are about their daughters. Mr. Towne hired me to follow her around and see that she didn't get into trouble. Without her realizing it, naturally."

"I'd say that was a pretty tall order."

"I'm hoping you'll help me."

The detective eyed him keenly. "You suggesting I don't arrest her?"

"That's right. There's bound to be a scandal if you do

which will only hurt an already sick girl and cost the store a valuable customer. Not to mention a suit for damages, most likely. Ansel Towne's a man who hits back when he's hurt, and hits hard. Wouldn't it be better for all concerned to handle this matter discreetly?"

"Sure, but what choice do I have?" Waters asked unhappily. "I can't stand here and let her rob us blind, I don't care whose daughter she is."

"Of course not. That's where I come in. We'll make an inventory of everything she takes and I'll settle the account in cash. Fair enough?"

Waters pondered the proposal, torn between duty and the possible consequences. As Fletch expected, prudence won the argument. "Screwiest thing I ever heard of," he grumbled. "Towne's the one who ought to have his head examined if you ask me, letting her get away with it. If she were my kid, I'd beat the living daylights out of her."

"The way it was explained to me, kleptomania is a disease—like measles."

"I've been in this business most of my life and I've yet to meet one honest-to-God kleptomaniac, just common thieves. And I say she's no exception." His disapproval voiced, Waters took out a small notebook. "Okay, one camera—$39.95."

"Add a man's billfold, alligator, I think—and a hot comb. She may not be very skillful, but she's fast."

Together, they trailed Timmy about the store. By the time she at last headed for the exit, the shopping bag was bulging and Waters had filled an entire page of his notebook. Fletch congratulated himself on enlisting the store detective as his unwitting confederate. With only luck and her own expertise to aid her, Timmy would surely have been apprehended almost immediately . . . and he wondered at Lionel Gann's willingness to send such an amateur on a job which called for a professional.

The tab came to $91.67. Fletch gave Waters the

hundred dollars he had retained for emergencies and insisted that he keep the change. "You've earned a good deal more than that. I'm sure Mr. Towne will think so too, when I tell him."

Waters sighed, too wise in the ways of the world to take much stock in gratitude once removed. "If you'd really like to thank me, just keep Miss Towne out of here in the future."

Timmy was waiting for him in the bus, her loot spread out on the seat beside her. "Hey, that wasn't such a jobber!" she exclaimed. "I almost went back for another shopping bag. Look at all this stuff! There must be two hundred dollars' worth, at least."

He didn't correct her inflated estimate. "The retail price means nothing. We'll be lucky to get fifty clams for the lot."

"That for real?" She conquered her disappointment. "Oh well, it's still not bad for openers. What's our next target?"

"Griffith Park. I've got eyes for a picnic."

"But we've just gotten started! Why should we stop so soon?"

"Because somebody may have spotted you. If they did, all the other stores will be alerted. No use pushing our luck." He didn't reveal another more valid reason, that he was out of cash to redeem her pilfering. "We'll play it cool—and under a tree at Griffith is the coolest place I can think of. Besides, you've earned yourself a little fun."

"Fun," Timmy repeated as if she had forgotten that such a word existed. "It does sound smokey. But I don't think Pappy would approve."

"In that case," Fletch said, starting the engine, "we won't invite him."

# Eight

"THANKS FOR A FANTASTIC DAY," Timmy murmured as they returned at dusk to the PTA's dismal lair. She sat close beside him with an intimacy nurtured during the long lazy afternoon. They had wandered through the nearly deserted park hand-in-hand, stopping to sprawl contentedly on the warm grass or to romp on the playground equipment like children half their age. "It was one of the best dates I've ever had."

"That doesn't say much for your social life."

"Well, actually, I've never done a lot of dating. Not compared to most people, anyway. You have, I suppose?"

"When other boys were chasing baseballs, I was chasing girls. And every now and then I even managed to catch one. Trouble is, I never knew what to do with her."

"Who you trying to kid?" she scoffed. "When it comes to girls, you know where the strings are and how to pull them. I know darn well you've been pulling mine."

"I don't read you—but I'm willing to learn."

She continued to pursue the subject. "I feel almost as if —oh, I don't know how to put it exactly—as if you're playing some kind of game with me, where you've programmed all the moves in advance and everything you say and do has a purpose."

Her intuition startled him but he could not admit its correctness. "I can see why you never had many dates. A fellow tries to be nice to you and right away you call him

66

Mr. Plastic."

"Oh, I didn't mean it like that! Don't be ticked off at me. I guess I'm just confused. I can't understand why you're bothering with me."

"What do you think today was all about, anyhow? Sure, I've been playing a game with you, the same game every guy plays with a girl he digs. Sorry if I was too subtle. I should have made it clearer by coming on like Injun."

Timmy shuddered. "Oh God, no! He turns my stomach."

"Well, there's one thing to be said for Injun. You'll never have to wonder why he's bothering with you. He'll lay it right on the line—and I do mean lay."

"I don't blame you for getting bent," she said in a small voice. "I didn't have any cause to say what I did. The truth is, I'm afraid of letting other people get too close. When I think it might be happening, I try to turn them off before I get hurt."

He decided that his pretended anger had served its purpose. "You don't have to be afraid of me, Timmy. Draw the line any place you like. I won't cross it without an invitation. On one condition."

"Oh?"

"That you remember I'm your friend, no matter what. Promise?"

"You drive a hard bargain," she said, snuggling against him. "But okay, if you insist." After a moment, she repeated thoughtfully, "No matter what. Hey, that sounds like you think there might be trouble ahead."

"Let me clue you out of my vast experience. There's always trouble ahead."

The others had already returned to the cellar, bringing with them the fruits of their labors, food and money and merchandise. Timmy's contribution, by far the largest and most valuable, was greeted with surprise and delight. Choogle, examining the loot with a practiced eye, concurred

67

with Fletch's previous estimate of its worth. "You done right well, child," he told her and the rest were equally complimentary. Only Gann showed no enthusiasm, perhaps because Timmy insisted in giving all the credit to Fletch.

"He's really something else," she bragged. "Without Fletch, I'd have messed up for sure."

"Didn't I call it?" Blossom reminded them. She hugged him, pleased that he had vindicated her sponsorship. "I told you he knew the score. There wasn't any cause to get antsy, see?"

"Oh, us of little faith!" Rufus Wren agreed. "When you two didn't show on time, the only question in our narrow minds was which slammer they'd booked you into. Right, Pappy?"

"So I blew one," Gann admitted with a trace of annoyance, the teacher caught in an error by his pupils. "So where does it say I'm infallible? I'm happy as hell to be proved wrong for once. You don't think I wanted the fuzz to jug them, do you?"

Fletch had a sudden intuition that the proper answer was yes. If so, it cleared up a mystery which had puzzled him earlier. Could Gann have deliberately given Timmy a task beyond her ability with the expectation that she would be apprehended? That made no sense on the surface—until he remembered Gann's remarks on the previous evening. A criminal record (first offenders were usually let off lightly, but the record remained) would serve to commit her irrevocably to the outlaws. Gann had permitted Fletch to accompany her, perhaps believing that his presence would make no difference, possibly hoping that the police would rid him of the newcomer. Machiavellian, yes, but consistent with Gann's character . . . and it seemed the only way to account for his barely concealed chagrin.

Fletch kept his suspicions to himself and accepted the

praise of the others, far simpler souls, with a shrug. If he had thwarted Gann's scheme, he didn't wish to make matters worse by rubbing his nose in it. "You think that's heavy? Wait till you see what I can do with a loaf of bread and a couple of fishes."

"How are you with pinto beans and bacon rind?" Wren inquired hopefully.

He was conscious of Gann's covert glances in his direction during supper. He thought he knew what was coming; he waited to discover how Gann would handle it. The messianic leader, devious as always, began by remarking that he considered it only fair to allow Fletch to take his pick of the stolen merchandise "as a token of our appreciation."

His subordinates greeted this proposal with puzzled expressions since they had assumed that, as with everything, the loot was the property of the group rather than any individual. Gann proceeded to enlighten them. "Fletch did fifty per cent of the work, at least. And he'll need some bread to get him wherever he's going."

"Going?" Blossom echoed. "I thought he was signing on with us."

"We all agreed that it was just a temporary arrangement. Fletch wanted a place to crash. I'm glad we were able to help him out. But I'm sure he has plans which don't include us."

"But why?" Timmy burst out in dismay. "I'll bet he'd stay if you asked him, Pappy. And we need him! You said yourself that we've got to recruit more righteous people if we're ever going to amount to anything. I move we make Fletch a member before some other tribe grabs him."

"Right on!" Rufus Wren chimed in. "Second the motion."

Fletch estimated that sentiment stood four-to-two in his favor with Gann and Injun opposed and Midge uncommitted. However, Gann had no intention of allowing the matter to come to a vote. He said sharply, "You're out of order, both of you. I formed the PTA, I command it—and I decide who stays and who goes. That includes everybody."

The naked threat converted Fletch's majority to a minority of one. Blossom cringed visibly. Wren, squirming, muttered, "I withdraw my second." Only Timmy remained steadfast. "I think that's brutal! Sure, we can't take in just anybody—but Fletch isn't just anybody! I mean, even if he hadn't been a wheel up at Berkeley, what he's done since he got here proves he belongs."

Gann sighed. "Let me explain it to you this way," he said, and slapped her across the mouth.

Timmy lurched back, more stunned by surprise than by the blow. She looked around bewildered, a child seeking succor. "Fletch?" she whimpered.

His instinctive reaction was sympathy but he quelled it immediately. He owed Timmy nothing—and to take her part against Gann would guarantee immediate expulsion. Or worse; he noted from the corner of his eye that Injun had drawn his knife. "Don't come crying to me," he told the girl coldly. "You bought that slap. There can only be one boss and Pappy's it."

Timmy shriveled like a dying flower. She fought to find her voice. "I'm—I'm sorry. I didn't mean to come on salty, honest I didn't."

Fletch turned to Gann. "I'm sorry too. I never intended to stir up trouble in the ranks. If there's anything I believe in it's tribal discipline."

Once again he could feel group sentiment shift. His forthright endorsement of their leader had won back the support of the majority. Even Gann appeared to thaw a trifle. "I'm glad to hear you say that. Maybe I've misjudged you."

Fletch smiled. "But you're still not sure."

"You bother me," Gann admitted. "Every time I think

70

I've got you cornered, you come off the wall. I can't decide just what you are. Will the real Chris Fletcher please stand up?"

"I thought you'd never ask. I can't blame you for wondering about me. I don't expect you to take me on faith. I earned my place up at Berkeley. I'd like the chance to earn my place here."

"Why?" Gann asked bluntly. "Seems to me that a guy with your track record would be looking for faster company."

Fletch put on a knowing expression. "Don't game me, Pappy. I've been here long enough to figure out this is where the action is. Well, I want a piece of it. And I think you can use a can-do type like me."

"For what?" Injun sneered. "Babysitting Timmy?"

"Cool it, Tonto," Fletch advised him. "My words are for the Great White Father."

Injun's eyes glittered. "You've got a big mouth, man. Keep flapping it at me and see what it buys you."

"Tell me the truth. Have you actually been scaring folks with that line?"

"Injun does have a point," Gann said. "So far all you've done is act as Timmy's security blanket. That doesn't make you Mr. Indispensable as far as I'm concerned. Maybe just the opposite."

"I've only been here twenty-four hours. I improve with age."

"I'll lay it on you plain, Fletch. The PTA was formed for a specific mission. The Co-op has given us a job to do, a heavy job, and I'm responsible for seeing it's done. I've got to have people I can depend on. Sure, I could use the kind of honcho you claim to be. But that's all it is, a claim. I can't take the risk of finding out when it's too late that you either can't or won't hack it."

His tone was one of finality but Fletch had no intention of allowing the matter to rest there. His own mission demanded that he not only retain his shaky seat at the guerrillas' Round Table but that he solidify it. "I read you loud and clear, Pappy. You mean that if I expect to hook on here, I've got to prove I'm more than just another pretty face. Okay, you're faded."

That wasn't what Gann meant and he knew it. But turning the dismissal into a dare put Gann on the defensive. He could not back away from it without seeming timid, a label no commander dares to wear. And so he parried. "I don't understand exactly what it is you're proposing."

Neither did Fletch—but having seized the ball, he had no choice except to run with it. "Suppose you put me to the test," he said slowly. "Make it anything you like. Within reason. If I score, I join the team. If I flunk it, I'll go quietly."

Gann shook his head. "No sale, Fletch. I don't have time to waste on dreaming up fraternity initiations."

"Then suppose I dream up my own initiation," Fletch suggested, desperately attempting to keep a foot in the door which was closing in his face. "All you need to do is watch. You have time enough for that, don't you?"

He sensed that the others, at least, were intrigued— what child can resist a show?—and that their leader, sensing it also, was hesitant to appear the wet blanket. Gann chose an alternate tactic. He threw the challenge back at the challenger. "Tell us more," he invited. "This test—what'd you have in mind?"

Nothing, of course; he was extemporizing to meet the demands of the moment. "How does hijacking the Sunset bus to Tijuana grab you?"

Gann smiled briefly. "If jokes are all you have to offer—"

"Give me some slack, man. I'll come up with something really flaming."

"But surely," Gann needled, "you wouldn't have suggested a test unless you had some little idea stirring, would you?"

"Of course not. I just haven't worked out all the details."

"A vague outline will do—just so we'll know you're not hyping us."

They were all watching him intently, friend and foe alike, waiting for him to make good his boast or to confess its hollowness. He stared back, his expression confident but his mind a blank; for once, invention had forsaken him. Like a magician, he groped in an empty top hat for a rabbit which was not there.

"Look at his face," Injun said contemptuously. "That's flop sweat!"

"Get off my case, creep," Fletch snapped, hoping to create a squabble which would buy more time.

The stratagem did not succeed. Gann, relentless as a terrier, refused him even a moment's respite. "Cool it. It's show-and-tell time, Fletch. Put a name on this so-called test of yours." As Fletch continued to hesitate, he smiled. "I'd say Injun called it right. You're a day late and a dollar short."

Dollar . . . Suddenly his frantic fingers closed on the elusive rabbit. He grinned around at his jury and so contagious was that grin that they returned it without knowing why. "I promised you a flaming caper and what I promise, I deliver. First, though, I'll have to raid the refrigerator for a few sticks of dynamite."

"A bomb?" Gann sighed with exaggerated disappointment. "Is that your best? Any clown can set off a bomb."

"Under COIN's headquarters?"

There was a stunned silence. "Say again?" Gann requested in an unbelieving whisper.

"Up till now all you've done with your bombs is trash a few banks and a police station or two. Big deal. That's like trying to kill a cat by pulling out its whiskers. I say let's gut the critter—and blowing up COIN is one way to do it. How does that grab you?"

The question was unnecessary; he could see that the audacious proposal had captured their imaginations. With the exception of Timmy's; she stared at him in wide-eyed consternation. "Not bad," Gann murmured. "If we could put Sugarman and his Gestapo out of business . . . How would you go about it?"

Fletch shrugged. "That's all she wrote—so far. If you like what you've heard to date, I'll work out the rest of it."

"Do that. But keep this in mind—nobody gets zapped. The Co-op wouldn't stand for it, not at this particular time. It doesn't fit in with our battle plan."

"Whatever's fair." He too had scruples against murder —though for different reasons, apparently—but there was no reason to tarnish his image by admitting it. "But since you're throwing in conditions, I'll add one of my own. I want a helper."

"You led us to believe this was going to be a one-man job."

"Right on. One man—and one woman. I'll need a decoy. I figure it should be Timmy."

She gasped, one hand flying to her mouth. "Why me? I couldn't do a thing like—" She stopped abruptly, recalling her previous chastisement, and finished in a barely audible voice, "I mean, I wouldn't know how."

Gann studied her through narrowed eyes. "I agree with you, Fletch. It should be Timmy. You make a good team, I hear—and she has something to prove, too. Use her any way you like. We can kill two birds with one stone."

"Mind rephrasing that? I don't like the way it sounds."

"How soon will you be able to get cracking?"

"Is now soon enough?" He rose and nudged Timmy with his foot. "Duty calls."

"Tonight?" she asked, startled.

"Yep. We're going into training. A delicate operation like this calls for absolute rapport between members of the strike force. So take up your sleeping bag and follow me."

Injun sprang to his feet. "Hey, what gives?"

"Timmy's going to be working under me. She'll need all the practice she can get. We'll pitch camp upstairs. No sense keeping you good people awake with our training exercises."

"Swive you, buddy! We don't allow no splitting off from the tribe. That's the rule. You'll stay here where we can watch you."

"Well, if that's what turns you on. But seeing as how I'm not really a member yet, I guess the rule doesn't apply to me."

"I don't give a damn about you! Bed down any place you like—but Timmy stays here."

"Maybe you didn't hear Pappy. He said I could use her any way I like."

Gann's eyes held veiled amusement. "Fletch is right," he told Injun. "If that's the way he wants to use her, I don't see any reason to object."

Injun swung away with a growl and took out his anger by kicking an apple box halfway across the cellar. Fletch seized Timmy's hand. "Save some breakfast for us. I expect to work up quite an appetite."

"If you need help, just holler," Choogle called after them. "Loud moans and gasps don't count."

Fletch reconnoitered the empty rooms on the floor above until he found one with a door he could lock. "To keep out the rats," he explained. "Particularly rats armed with knives." He fastened the candle to the wooden floor with its drippings and spread his sleeping bag beside it. "Make yourself at home."

Timmy continued to stand near the door, clutching her own sleeping bag like a shield. The camaraderie of the afternoon had completely vanished. Studying her, he asked quietly, "Problems?"

"I don't know what you mean."

"I seem to detect a certain disapproval, bordering on utter loathing."

"What difference does it make? You're getting what you want, aren't you?"

"Which question do you want me to answer first?"

"Oh, you're so damn witty!" she burst out. "Everything's a joke to you—particularly me! You sure had me going. I thought you were something special, someone I could really relate to. Boy, was I ever lame! When I needed you down there, all I got was a kick in the teeth."

Fletch sighed. "How soon they forget! May I remind you what you promised me just a few short hours ago?"

"I promised, well, to remember you're my friend, no matter what," she said unwillingly. "But—"

"No buts. I'm holding you to your promise. You missed the point of that little charade downstairs. If I'd backed you against Pappy, he'd have had the excuse he wanted to boot me out. I'm walking a tightrope, baby. One slip and I've bought it. So I let you take the slap in the face instead of me because you could survive it and I couldn't."

"I don't believe you. You're very clever at making excuses but actions speak louder than words."

"Wait a minute. I want to write that down."

"Go ahead—laugh at me! That doesn't change the facts. I wasn't the only one who made a promise this afternoon. You promised you wouldn't force me, that you wouldn't—" With sudden contempt, she flung her sleeping bag down beside his. "Oh, what's the use! Let's stop yapping and get on with it." She groped for the zipper of her dress.

"You think I hauled you up here to bang you?"

"Now what would ever make me think that?" she retorted sarcastically. "Cut it out, won't you? You don't have to game me any longer. You've already gotten Pappy's blessing—isn't that enough? Come on. The sooner it's over, the sooner I can get to sleep."

Fletch picked up her sleeping bag and threw it into a far corner of the room. "Pleasant dreams."

Timmy halted in the act of stepping out of the dress. She stared at him, squinting to read his expression in the flickering candlelight. "I don't get it," she said slowly.

"That's right. Not tonight and not from me."

"Then why did you make me think, make everybody believe that—"

"I figured that if I didn't stake my claim, Injun would. You've held him off about as long as you can without help. But maybe I should have minded my own business."

"Are you kidding? Oh, Fletch, I'm so ashamed of dumping on you!" She ran to him and threw her arms about his neck and kissed him gratefully.

Her lips were sweeter than he wished them to be, her body softer and more inviting. Aroused against his will, he prolonged the embrace past what mere forgiveness demanded. For a moment she remained pliant in his grasp; then he felt her stiffen. He released her with a laugh. "Wrong again, babe."

"About what?"

"About me. Tell the truth. Didn't the thought cross your mind just now that oh-oh! maybe you'd better not trust this joker too far, after all?"

A sheepish smile was his answer. "I guess you think I'm pretty weird—coming on like Little Nell in one of those old-time melodramas. I mean, who am I kidding, right? A virgin I ain't. It's just that, well, sex is still important to me."

"You won't catch me knocking it either."

"What I'm trying to say is that it has to mean something. It should be—beautiful. And I know it can be 'cause I've been there. With Ken. That's why I can't stand for a scuz like Injun—"

"Or me."

"Oh, no! I think, with you—well, it might not be so bad."

"Gee, thanks."

She looked stricken. "There I go again. That sounded terrible, didn't it? You're the last person in the world I should chop."

"I'm putting it all on the account. One of these days I'll collect. With interest."

She assumed he was still talking about sex. "You're almost too good to be true," she said slowly, coming closer to the truth than she could imagine. "What'd I ever do to deserve you?"

He kept his tone light. "Wouldn't it be a brutal world if we only got what we deserve?"

"Isn't it?" she replied somberly. Then she managed an answering smile. "Present company excepted. If it could always be like this, just you and me . . . But it can't. I'll lose you like I lost Ken."

And, Fletch thought, like I lost Curt. "Oh, I'm a hard man to lose. There may come a day when you'll wish I wasn't."

He concluded the conversation by extinguishing the candle. They undressed in the darkness and traded good nights. After that, there was silence and he decided that she had fallen asleep. Her whisper startled him. "Fletch— you still awake?"

"Yeah, I'm awake."

"Do you mind if I come over there? I'd sleep better being close to you." Permission granted, she slid her bag next to his and groped in the darkness for his hand. "Now I feel safe," she murmured. "You won't let the bogeyman get me, will you?"

For the first time he felt a twinge of remorse at how he was conning her. For the first time he saw her not as a pawn to be maneuvered but as a vulnerable confused child,

78

frightened of the darkness that had nothing to do with the night. "That's right," he said gently. "I won't let the bogeyman get you."

And that was the biggest con of all. He had gained a trust he meant to betray and that might, ultimately, cost her life. With a guardian like him, who needed a bogeyman?

# Nine

IN THE MORNING he felt otherwise, of course. He was able once more to drive away compassion with the whip of vengeance. Timmy and her comrades had shown no compassion for Curt. They had executed him without compunction and without remorse. Quid pro quo; he came not to forgive but to punish.

Their return to the cellar, hand-in-hand, was greeted matter-of-factly. There was a complete absence of sly innuendo and knowing smiles. Timmy might still invest sex with some significance but the others did not. Consequently it was no more worth discussing than a bowel movement. Injun came the closest to expressing prurient interest by wondering sarcastically if they'd been too busy to work out the details of the bombing.

"It's shaping up," Fletch assured him. "And thanks for asking. It's good to know you're concerned."

"How about clueing the rest of us in on the way you mean to handle it?" Injun persisted, making the suggestion sound like a dare.

"Okay, it's still rough but here's the skinny. Timmy and I invade COIN five minutes before quitting time. She stays in the lobby while I go directly to General Sugarman's private office. I drop the bomb on the old fart's desk, stroll back to the lobby—and we leave quietly just before they lock the doors."

They were all staring at him incredulously. "He's

flipped out!" Injun declared with a certain amount of satisfaction. "Hey, dummy, what do you think Sugarman's goons are gonna be doing?"

"Looking at Timmy. Oh, I forgot to mention that she'll be riding an elephant. Only thing I haven't figured out yet is where to get the elephant." He shrugged. "I warned you it was still rough."

Rufus Wren exploded with laughter. After a moment the rest joined in with the exception of Injun who flushed in tardy recognition that he was being mocked. "You're about as funny as the clap, Fletcher."

"I won't argue with an authority. But suppose you stay in your field and quit butting into mine."

Gann intervened to preserve the peace. "All right, you've made your point. We'll stop hassling you. That's an order, Injun. And here's one for you, Fletch. Don't be such a smart ass."

Fletch accepted the rebuke with a smile and began to discuss the bomb with Blossom and Midge, who would be responsible for its construction. Injun, however, lapsed into a surly silence. He left without eating breakfast and without saying goodbye. "Villagers, beware," Rufus Wren murmured when he was safely out of earshot. "The monster is loose."

"He'll cool down," Gann predicted. But when the meal was finished, he motioned Fletch to join him on the other side of the cellar. "You've been shafting Injun pretty good. Granted, he's an easy target but I'm afraid you're overdoing it."

"Thanks for the warning."

"Actually, it was more of a question. Why are you deliberately provoking him? And don't say you aren't."

"You must have doped that out. We've both got eyes for the same thing."

"Timmy?"

"The number two spot in the pecking order. I figure I

deserve it more than he does. Injun figures just the opposite. So naturally we're bound to tangle."

"You're forgetting something. I decide the pecking order here."

"I wouldn't have it any other way. Because, given the choice between Injun and me, you've got to choose me."

"What makes you so sure?"

"All Injun has to offer is muscle. That's fine up to a point. But there comes a time when you need brains more than brawn—and in the brains department he rates about minus three."

"He's been very useful to me. He still is."

"So use him. I'm not suggesting that you read him out of the party. All I ask is that you keep an open mind and give natural selection a chance."

Gann promised only that he would think it over; however, Fletch felt that he had scored a victory. Gann and Injun together represented the real strength of the PTA. If he could drive a wedge between them, the tribe would disintegrate. The danger, of course, in pitting one against the other was that he might get caught in the middle. His role called for fancy footwork but it was an art in which he'd had plenty of practice. Which was more than could be said for his more immediate task, that of blowing up a building.

"We've got work to do," he told Timmy. "And promises to keep."

Rufus Wren bummed a ride with them as far as the public library, where he was researching a term paper on the minor Elizabethan poets for a student at USC. Wren supplied reports on any subject at $3.50 per page, tailored to the professor's taste and the pupil's past performance, with a passing grade guaranteed. He had more customers than he could handle and was, in fact, considering hiring a couple of assistant ghosts to meet the demand.

"You know what that makes you? A bloody capitalist."

Wren giggled. "I suppose that's one way of looking at

it. I prefer to believe that I'm undermining the Toppies by subverting their educational processes."

His fees, like the smaller amounts the others earned or stole, went into the guerrilla organization's war chest. The PTA itself retained only a tiny percentage of the money and the individual members none at all. Neither Wren nor Timmy knew to what use the Co-op put it (though presumably Gann did) but they assumed it was to equip the underground army for the battle ahead. Fletch, more cynical than they, couldn't help but wonder whether someone somewhere wasn't profiting handsomely from their revolutionary fervor. The history of other revolutions demonstrated that such was more often the rule than the exception.

They dropped Wren off at the downtown library and drove out to the San Fernando Valley where COIN had its headquarters. Fletch had never seen it before; Sugarman preferred that he have no direct connection with the organization or its other employees. The imposing white marble building, set amid a small park atop a wooded hill, was Grecian in style. Had the trees which surrounded it been olives instead of eucalyptus it might have been a temple consecrated to Zeus or Apollo. Yet there were computers in the basement and a radio transmitter on the roof, both capable of miracles which the ancient gods would have envied. Into COIN flowed a constant stream of information, battle reports from a dozen fronts of the subterranean war. From COIN flowed a constant, but smaller, stream of intelligence summaries, assessing the enemy's strength, analyzing his actions and—as far as human and electronic brains, working together, could manage it—predicting his intentions. Many of the professionals in the field scoffed publicly at COIN as a group of clumsy albeit well-meaning amateurs. Privately, a few hesitated to avail themselves of COIN's services when the need arose.

Fletch parked within sight of the temple's colonnaded

entrance. For a while, he and Timmy sat in silence, staring at their objective. "I'd give a hundred bucks to know what the inside of that joint looks like," he said longingly, knowing full well that she had been born there.

"Fork it over, buster. My grandfather built that house out of his ill-gotten gains and monumental bad taste." She noted his exaggerated incredulity. "Didn't Pappy clue you? My daddy's Ansel Towne. He's one of the wheels behind COIN. He gave the place to them." She added scornfully, "It'd been standing empty ever since we moved up to Trousdale Estates. A real white elephant. Daddy made himself look good and took a hefty tax write-off at the same time."

"So you're Ansel Towne's daughter," Fletch murmured as though he found it hard to believe. "Hey, babe, you must be rich!"

"Only in money."

"Any qualms about trashing the ancestral home?"

"No. I've always hated it."

"Why? It's nothing but a building."

"Well, just look at it. What sort of a place is that for a kid to grow up in? It's about as homey as Forest Lawn. But the worst part was that living there made me someone special when all I wanted was to be like everyone else. I guess you can't dig that, can you?"

"Maybe not. My ambition was always to be someone special."

Timmy sighed. "What'd they call you in school? Fletch? Chris?"

"Handsome. For obvious reasons."

"They called me Money Bags—or M.B. for short— or sometimes just Bags. And always as a putdown, like calling a Jew a kike or a black a nigger. I wasn't the prettiest child in the world, I was overweight, I stammered . . . You get the picture. I'd have had it rough enough even without being Miss Timothea Towne, the richest kid in

84

Southern California. The more I tried to be just one of the gang, the worse it was. I never had any really close friends. I made the other kids uncomfortable. I mean, when you ride the bus, how can you relate to somebody who has a chauffeured limousine? And later on, if some boy should work up enough nerve to ask me for a date, there was always my bodyguard trailing along. Daddy was scared to death of kidnappers. God, I almost used to wish that somebody would grab me, carry me off and never bring me back! Especially after Mom died and there wasn't even anyone to come home to."

"You ever try telling this to your old man?"

"Yeah. You know what his brilliant solution was? An appointment twice a week with the best psychiatrist in Beverly Hills. Daddy's second wife was very large on Freud. Or was it his third? I forget. It doesn't matter, anyway. All analysis did for me was to give the other kids another reason to turn me off."

"I want a list of their names and addresses. I'll punch them all in the mouth."

"Where were you when I needed you? I think I was the loneliest girl in the world. Did you ever play jump rope?"

"I was block champion at Double Dutch."

"Then you probably remember 'On the mountain stands a lady, who she is I do not know . . .' "

"Sure. What's the rest of it? 'Dressed from head to toe in diamonds, why she cries, I do not know.' Right?"

"Uh-huh. Well, I knew who that lady was. It was me. And I knew why she was crying in spite of all her diamonds." Timmy seemed close to tears now; she forced a scornful laugh. "Hey, how did we get into the hearts-and-flowers scene, anyway? That dumb lady stopped sniveling and came down off her damn mountain a long time ago."

He was not deceived by the bravado. Timmy was still that lonely girl, grown older but no less vulnerable, still crying to a world which found her tears incomprehensible.

Seen in that light, her rebellion became understandable, perhaps even inevitable. She had recoiled from everything —family, fortune, society itself—which she blamed for her unhappiness. Yet Fletch hesitated to hold Ansel Towne or his money entirely accountable. Such a curbstone condemnation was too easy; the real answer was seldom that simple. Furthermore, he reminded himself, Timmy's trauma was no concern of his.

So he kept his tone light. "You think you had a miserable childhood? I was the youngest of four kids, and the only boy. We were so poor I had to wear my sisters' hand-me-downs. Why, I was twelve years old before I owned a pair of jeans with the zipper in front!"

This time her laugh was genuine. "You seem to have made a bitchen recovery. What's your secret?"

"I got rid of my neurosis the day I burned my bra. That's where Women's Lib stole the idea. Maybe bombing the old plantation will do the same for you. Describe the layout to me. What's the first thing I see after I open that big front door?"

Timmy knew the mansion intimately. At his direction, she drew a floor plan of each level with special emphasis on possible hiding places and escape routes. As to the security measures if any that COIN presently employed, however, she was uninformed. There was some sort of a burglar alarm system but how extensive and how sophisticated she did not know. Armed guards? Perhaps; she wasn't sure.

"Let's assume that there are, just to be on the safe side. And let's also assume that they've beefed up the alarm system with electronic gimmicks to protect their expensive equipment. Computers aren't cheap and neither, I gather, is your old man."

"I'm afraid you may be right. Daddy does dig that sort of toy. What do we do about it, Fletch?"

"Beats me. Do you suppose Pappy would agree to let us mail the bomb to COIN in a plain brown wrapper?"

Gann received their scouting report that evening with a certain amount of impatience. "Sure, they've got some kind of an alarm system and armed guards, too. What the hell did you expect—a big sign saying, 'Welcome, Fletch, please place bomb here'?"

"I'm only trying to impress you with the difficulties. Aren't you impressed? I am."

Injun saw a chance to discredit his rival. "I say you're trying to jam it. Like I thought—you're chicken."

Timmy leapt to the defense. "That's a lie! Fletch is not chicken."

"You bet I'm not," Fletch agreed. "By the way, anybody like to buy a dozen eggs?"

Gann's lips curved in a pained smile. "All you need is a laugh track—and it's 'Welcome to the Chris Fletcher Show, folks!' Give me some brevity instead of levity for a change. Have you and Timmy worked out a plan or haven't you?"

"You bet we have. Lay it on them, partner."

She blinked. "All I know is that you bought a tool box and a pair of coveralls."

"Okay, then I'll lay it on. The tool box is to carry the bomb in. The coveralls are to make me look like a guy who has a reason to carry the tool box. According to Timmy, the employees' lounge is in the basement and in said lounge is a soft drink dispenser. Tomorrow afternoon I'm going to show up to repair it."

"But how do you know it's broken?" Blossom objected.

"Did you ever see a vending machine that wasn't, at least half the time? Anyway, all I'll know is that my company received a complaint and sent me to check it out. So I fiddle around with the thing for a while and leave, forgetting to take the tool box with me. A few hours after that—boom! Any questions? Yes, the gentleman in the balcony."

Wren lowered his hand. "What if they have somebody

watching you while you work? Won't they figure out that you're not really a repairman?"

"Who can tell a real repairman from a phony these days? Next question."

"Suppose whoever you talk to knows there's nothing wrong with the machine and tells you not to bother?" Midge asked.

"So what is it going to hurt to let me look it over, at least? Here I made a special trip all the way from downtown and how come they called me anyway if there wasn't anything wrong? If anyone asks who called me, why, I'm just the serviceman. I go where the dispatcher tells me. The main thing is to play it a little snotty as if they're lucky I even bothered to come, so don't bug me."

"But when you don't come back—" Choogle began.

"Nobody'll give it a second thought. That time of day, they'll all be concentrating on finishing their own work and getting the hell out of there. If someone does notice the tool box, he won't mention it because that might make it his responsibility." Fletch looked around. "Any more questions? If not, that concludes this evening's performance. Feel free to applaud."

"I got a question," Injun said loudly. "What about Timmy? I mean, she was supposed to be in this with you. All I've heard is me, me, me. Not one word about her."

"Injun, I'm delighted to learn it's not true what they say about you. You're not as stupid as you look. Timmy's part in this is to sit quietly in the lobby while I'm working below. In case anything goes wrong, she throws a screaming fit to distract the defense while I cut out in the confusion."

"I get it. If you pull it off, you take all the credit. And if you blow it, Timmy's left holding the bag."

"Which bothers you more?" Fletch inquired sweetly. "Timmy holding the bag or me getting the credit?"

Injun had no talent for repartee; he looked to Gann for

support. For the first time, the bearded leader did not choose to oblige, an encouraging indication that Injun had suffered a loss of status. "I get a little weary of the jealousy bit," he observed and there was no doubt to whom the reproof was directed. "Fletch, you make this mission sound real simple. Maybe too simple. General Sugarman's no dummy. Somehow I can't see him leaving himself so wide open."

"Remember Pearl Harbor. The top brass there couldn't believe that the Japs would have the chutzpah to attack it. I'm betting that the same type military genius is running COIN."

"Well, if chutzpah is all it takes, you're home free. But throw in a little caution too, okay? What I'm trying to say is that you'll be a hell of a lot better off if you remember to run scared."

"How's this?" Fletch held up a shaking hand.

The evening concluded in the same fashion as the one previously, with Fletch and Timmy excusing themselves to go upstairs and Injun glowering but unable to prevent them. "I can't get over it," Timmy mused. "The way things have changed since you got here. I mean, the way you've cut Injun down to size and even made Pappy take a back seat. And without ever once losing your cool."

"All the returns aren't in yet."

A worried frown replaced her smile. "You do think everything's going all right, don't you?"

"Ever hear the one about the guy who fell off the skyscraper? Each floor he passed, he yelled, 'I'm doing fine so far!' That's me, baby."

"That's not you at all," Timmy said positively. "I think I'm finally beginning to figure you out, Fletch. You don't fall off anything. You jump. And when you do, you always have a reason and you always know exactly where you're going to land."

"Okay, suppose you tell me."

"I haven't gotten that far yet. All I know for sure is that you're not what you'd like other people to believe you are."

Once again her intuition surprised him—and, once again, he chose to hide behind a smoke screen of pretended irritation. "Nobody wants the world to know what he's really like, for God's sake! Lay off the analysis, will you? When I need my character read, I'll buy a fortune cookie."

Chastened, Timmy fell silent. However, he was shortly given a second and much greater surprise. Watching him strip off his shirt preparatory to retiring, she murmured, "Funny."

"Sorry, dear. It's the only body I've got."

"Oh, you're gorgeous and you know it. I was just wondering . . . Fletch, you don't happen to have an older brother, do you?"

The question nearly took his breath away and gave an unwarranted sharpness to his reply. "No. Why?"

"You remind me of somebody, that's all. Not in looks so much—though there is a certain resemblance. It goes deeper than that. There was this fellow who was with us a while back . . . I didn't get to know him very well but he was a lot like you."

He had no doubt whom she meant. "Yeah?" he replied cautiously. "In what way?"

"It's hard to describe. About the only way I can put it is that I got the same vibrations from him that I get from you. And because he told me once that he had a brother—"

"And I'm telling you that I don't."

"Well, you don't have to get all bent out of shape about it," she retorted. "I just thought you'd be interested. Sorry I even mentioned it."

Shock had caused him to overreact; he sought to repair the mistake. "I am interested, Timmy. Who is this guy? I'd like to meet him and compare vibes."

"We called him Vince but I guess his name was really Curt. Curt Orr. At least, that's what it said in the papers."

"How'd he make the papers?"

"He bought the farm." She shuddered. "I really am sorry I brought it up. Forget I said anything, okay? We're not supposed to talk about him, even to each other."

"Good idea," he agreed with an indifference he was far from feeling. "Counting casualties is bad for morale." He ached to probe further. But Timmy could not add anything of significance to what he already knew and to badger her for details might cause her to wonder and, ultimately, to suspect.

Or did she suspect already? It seemed odd that she would compare him, her trusted friend, with Curt, her mortal enemy. And she had spoken of Curt without rancor but with sorrow . . . Had she been trying to trick him into an admission? Had others also noted the resemblance and was this Gann's devious way of trapping him? It didn't seem likely. And yet . . . My God! he thought. Could it be possible that *she* is really conning *me*?

# Ten

THE QUESTION CONTINUED to haunt him throughout the night and most of the following day. Self-confidence bordering upon hubris is essential to the successful con artist. This afternoon he had a date to bomb COIN's headquarters. The assignment hadn't worried him before. But if he had lost his touch, like an athlete gone stale . . . Gann had admonished him to run scared. Last night he'd scorned the advice; today he had no difficulty accepting it.

As it turned out, the operation went off without a hitch. The employees at COIN were a surprisingly friendly lot and the headquarters scarcely the security-conscious fortress he expected. It apparently never occurred to anyone that they constituted a prime target—or that the young man who showed up to repair the soft drink dispenser might be an enemy saboteur. Shaving off his beard helped, no doubt, but on the whole Fletch encountered less suspicion than he would have found attempting to cash a check at a strange bank. On the contrary, he was treated with such cheerful courtesy that he felt ashamed of the deception he practiced. He might well have abandoned the whole scheme—if, in fact, there had been anything to abandon.

To sell himself to the guerrillas, he must plant the bomb . . . but he had no intention of permitting the bomb to explode.

Two courses were open to him. The first was to disarm

the bomb, a relatively unsophisticated device consisting of dynamite, blasting cap and alarm clock, constructed from a basic recipe found in the *Anarchist's Cookbook*. Its manufacturers, Blossom and Midge, handled it with confidence. Fletch, who knew far less about explosives, preferred not to handle it at all. He wisely chose the second option.

There was a telephone in the deserted lounge. He dialed 9 to get an outside line and rang the private number at which Sugarman had promised he could be reached day or night. Fletch did not know where the other instrument was located; he suspected it might even be in the same building.

His commander was relieved to hear from him. "I've been sweating you out, boy. Especially after that fiasco at MacArthur Park."

"Did you square things with that cop I slugged?"

"I couldn't do that without spilling the whole story— and I want to keep that our little secret." Sugarman obviously considered the incident unimportant. "What have you got to report?"

"Well, you were right, General. Something big's brewing. Don't ask me what because I haven't been able to find out yet. Anyway, that's not why I called you." He eyed the stairs from which interruption might come at any moment. "Time's short, so listen carefully. There's a bomb planted beside the soft drink dispenser in COIN's basement."

Sugarman's voice went up a full octave. "A bomb! What are you talking about? How do you know?"

"Because I just put it there."

"You put it—" Sugarman sounded in danger of strangling. "What the hell kind of a game are you playing, Orr?"

"The name is Fletcher and it's no game. The bomb is set to go off at nine o'clock tonight. I want you to arrange for it to be discovered before then."

"I'll have the sheriff's bomb squad on it in ten minutes."

"No, you won't. You're going to wait until eight o'clock before you call the cops. Then don't give your name. Just tell them that the bomb's in a tool box that was left this afternoon by a fellow pretending to be a repairman—and that they'd better get out there and disarm it before it blows up. Oh, and warn them the lid is booby-trapped. Is that clear?"

It wasn't precisely the tone one took with a general officer and Sugarman reacted accordingly. "Not by a damn sight, mister! And until you give me some good reason—"

Footsteps sounded on the stairs; someone was descending to the lounge. "I can't talk any longer," Fletch said hastily. "But if you need a reason, how's this? My way is the only way you'll get what you want. Yes or no, General?"

Angry or not, Sugarman was a man of quick decisions. "Yes!" he snapped. "But you better know what you're doing because I sure as hell don't."

The footsteps belonged to Miss Harter, the flirtatious secretary who had escorted him to the basement lounge. "Not finished yet?" she asked. "Darn, I'd do anything for a Coke."

"No way. But I'll sure keep it in mind for the future."

She was young enough to be amused by the innuendo but old enough to realize it was not to be taken seriously. "That kind of talk could get you in a whole lot of trouble."

"I certainly hope so." He hung an Out of Order sign on the dispenser door. "I've got to run back to the plant for a new part. Pass the word not to mess with the gizmo while I'm gone, okay? You might blow a fuse."

"Hey," she called after him. "Aren't you forgetting something?"

"My goodbye kiss?"

"Your tool box," she enlightened him, pointing to where it nestled beside the machine.

Fletch hesitated on the stairs. "Might as well leave it here till I get back. The darn thing's too heavy to lug around."

Timmy was sitting in the lobby which had formerly been the foyer of her home. She was pretending to study the application for employment he had directed she obtain from the receptionist. Their eyes met, he winked and saw the anxiety drain out of her face as if a stopper had been removed. But she remembered his instructions and did not speak to him or turn her head to watch him depart.

Fletch waited in the bus for her to join him. "What took you so long?" she demanded in a voice shaky with relief. "I thought you were never coming out, I was sure they'd caught you—"

"To tell the truth, I was having such a swinging time with Miss Harter that I couldn't tear myself away."

"You think I don't believe it? I saw how you gave her the eye. Big deal! I could make you drool too if I wore clothes seven sizes too small for me."

"Why, Timmy! I do believe you're jealous."

Her mouth flew open to issue an indignant denial, then closed slowly. She sat silently for a moment, staring at him with startled eyes. "My God!" she said at last.

"Please, no idolatry. A simple 'your majesty' will suffice."

"I am jealous. I swore I wouldn't let it happen but it has. I'm actually hung on you, Fletch." Timmy shook her head wonderingly. "How about that!"

"Why so surprised? I warned you I was habit forming."

"But do you . . ." She hesitated.

"Do I groove on you too? Well, what do you think?"

"I think," she said slowly, "that you could—if you'd let yourself. What's stopping you, Fletch?"

"There you go again," he parried, "trying to analyze

me. You're wrong, Timmy. Nothing's stopping me. I've just been waiting for you to flash the green light."

She eyed him searchingly. "Do you really mean that?" He could see that the glib explanation did not entirely convince her—but because she wished to believe it, she did so. She took his hand and put it to her lips, solemnly, as if plighting her troth. "I'll do anything you say, be anything you want. All you have to do is love me a little."

He grinned, his self-confidence fully restored. "You've got yourself a deal." The con was not only alive but flourishing and he'd been a fool to doubt it. Timmy had succumbed to it; Lionel Gann and the rest of Curt's murderers would follow.

So he returned to the PTA's cellar hideout in jaunty triumph—and was chagrined to find no hero's welcome awaiting him. The little army seemed oddly subdued, even a trifle hostile. Only Gann returned his greeting. The others remained silent.

Fletch looked around, craning to scrutinize the shadowy corners of the room. "Okay, where is it?"

"Where's what?"

"The body. I have the feeling I stumbled into a wake." Gann chuckled. "That could be."

The chuckle, almost a snarl, disturbed Fletch. From the corner of his eye, he noted that Injun had drifted to a position behind him, as if to cut off a retreat. Something was wrong but since he could not imagine what, he maintained his cheerful façade. "Well, isn't anybody going to ask how things went?"

"Sure. How did things go?"

"COIN welcomed us with open arms. Even as I speak, our bomb is ticking merrily away in their basement." He paused, waiting for approval; it was not forthcoming. "I can give you a blow-by-blow account if you're interested but it's hardly worth it. The job's done and all we have to do now is to watch the big finish on the late news."

96

"I've got a better idea," Gann said silkily. "TV's fine—but there's nothing like being there. We've decided to drive out to the Valley and catch the show live."

Fletch cleared his throat. "Isn't that a little risky?"

"We don't have to park on COIN's front porch. When your bomb blows, we'll be able to hear it a mile away. Or should I say, if your bomb blows?"

"What are you talking about? Why shouldn't the bomb blow?"

"I was at a meeting of the Co-op this afternoon. I told them what you were doing. They agreed it was a boss idea. They had just one question: Who the hell is this Chris Fletcher? Nobody had ever heard of you. That worried me because, between us, we know just about everybody who's anybody in the movement. So I phoned a friend of mine up at Berkeley—and you know what? He'd never heard of Chris Fletcher either."

Fletch hoped his laugh sounded genuine. "I get it. You've put me back in police uniform again, right?"

"The thought did occur to us."

"Go to your room, all of you. Why didn't you ask me what name I used at Berkeley? It wasn't Chris Fletcher, that's just an alias. You'll find I was registered at Cal under my square handle of Fletcher Christian Kantarski," He winked at Rufus Wren. "*Mutiny on the Bounty* was my mom's favorite picture. The Gable-Laughton version."

"I should hope so," Wren said. "The Brando thing was a travesty."

"Very smooth," Gann murmured, refusing to be put off. "And it might even be true. But the fact remains that we have only your word for it."

"Ask your friend to check me out."

"It wouldn't necessarily prove a thing. I mean, there could well be a Kantarski on record—but who's to say you're actually that Kantarski?" He shook his head. "We'll let the bomb decide. If you're what you claim to be, it'll go off on schedule. But if you're not—if you're an undercover pig or narc—you'll have made some arrangements to stop it."

"I don't buy that. Suppose Blossom and Midge goofed in putting the bomb together. Suppose the timing device doesn't—"

"Man, you're supposing yourself into an early grave," Gann interrupted with sudden harshness. Fletch felt something prick the nape of his neck and knew without looking that it was Injun's knife. "I'm willing to give you a fair trial, but if that isn't acceptable to you . . ."

He saw Timmy's horrified face and, with an effort, managed to give her a reassuring smile. "Since you put it that way, you're absolutely right. We'll let the bomb decide. Let's get stepping." He had not yet devised a plan to escape when the bombing was aborted but his chances were infinitely better behind the wheel of the Volkswagen than here in the cellar.

Gann had come to the same conclusion. "You stay. Timmy too, since she's on trial along with you. Injun will keep you company while we're gone. Choogle, get his car keys."

Nor was that the extent of it. Fletch's hands were bound behind his back with the clothesline and the other end of the rope secured to a floor joist, with barely enough slack to permit him to sit uncomfortably on one of the wooden boxes. Timmy, considered less of a danger though no less a captive, was not bound.

"Nearly eight," Gann observed. "We should be back between nine-thirty and ten if all goes well." He smiled. "Or even if it doesn't."

"Mind telling Injun that it's bad manners to hold the execution before the jury returns its verdict?"

"Injun has his orders."

"Drive carefully!" Fletch called after them. "The life you save may be mine."

98

Injun uttered a derisive snort. He sat cross-legged on the cellar floor, facing his prisoners, took out a whetstone and began to hone his already sharp knife. He looked up from his labor to catch Fletch's eye. "Think about it," he advised, moving the blade in a small glittering circle. "I want to see you sweat."

"Just tell me when you've had enough. I don't care to overwork my glands."

"Fun-ny. Always full of jokes. Two more hours and I'll see what else you're full of."

"I think it's scuzzy!" Timmy burst out with a mixture of fear and indignation. "We did everything Pappy wanted, didn't we?"

"Don't let it stoke you," Fletch admonished. "Everything's going to be all right." He was a long way from believing it. His original scheme had called for the police to disarm the bomb, with Injun—who customarily absented himself from the cellar following supper—to get the blame as the informer. The first part of the scheme was still operative . . . but now there would be no doubt as to the identity of the informer. It remained for him to construct a new and equally convincing scenario but his mind was a blank, devoid of inspiration.

Timmy, who understood none of this, shook her head angrily. "Oh, I know it's going to be all right, eventually. It just fractures me that they don't trust us."

"To trust is to perish. The Gospel According to Pappy."

Timmy appealed to their jailer. "Injun, you know he isn't going to run away. Be a good guy and cut him loose."

"Well, now, I might just do that—if you asked me real nice. Come on over here and let's discuss it."

"Stay away from him," Fletch warned. "You know what he's got in mind, don't you? And I guarantee that cutting me loose is at the bottom of his list."

Injun rose to his feet and stretched lazily, the muscles of

his bare chest rippling in the candlelight like tiny waves on a bronze pond. "Could be the man's right, baby. I been figuring to ball you sooner or later. Would have before this if it hadn't been for him. But it looks like the time done come."

Timmy backed away. He sauntered after her. "Hell, it won't hardly take no time at all. And it only hurts if you fight it."

"I'll tell Pappy!"

"You do that. And I'll tell Pappy it was your own idea, that you tried to make a deal for the boy friend. You did, didn't you?" He beckoned with both hands. "Come to Injun. See what a real man's like."

Fletch said harshly, "You're forgetting something. When that bomb goes off, I'm going to be the real man around here. You touch her and I'll total you."

"Is that a fact?" Yet the threat registered; Injun stopped his indolent pursuit of the woman to regard him beadily. "Maybe I got the answer to that too." He used the tip of the knife to raise Fletch's chin to an unnatural position. "Suppose you was to try and make a break for it. I'd have to stop you, right? Then you wouldn't be around to total nobody. Pappy might not be too jazzed about it but what's done is done."

"Timmy would still be around. Maybe you're figuring to kill her too—but I can't see Pappy buying two dead bodies."

There was a long silence during which he could feel the knife point dig deeper into the soft flesh of his throat. Injun removed the blade with a laugh. "I can wait. I'm gonna have my fun—both ways—before the night's through, anyhow."

But as he turned away, he kicked the box from under his captive. Fletch toppled backward. The rope secured to the joist stopped him short of the floor with a jolt that nearly dislocated both shoulders. He dangled there for an instant, dizzy with pain, until he could gain his feet and relieve the tension.

"Sorry about that," Injun apologized. "Didn't hurt you, did I?"

Timmy rushed forward to replace the box and to ease Fletch onto it once more. "Don't provoke him," she whispered, advice which he found somewhat ridiculous under the circumstances. "He'll get his as soon as Pappy comes back. God, I can hardly wait!"

Fletch could. He asked the time and was disconcerted to learn that it was nearly nine; one hour left, maybe less. Timmy, noticing his grimace, asked him if he hurt a lot. He admitted he did but the ache in his shoulders was nothing compared to the throbbing in his head as he tried to devise an escape from the disaster which came closer with each tick of the clock.

Time is immutable; it is only man's imagination which causes it to rush or to dawdle. The hour between 9 and 10 P.M. was no longer and no shorter than any other. To Injun, studying his prey with hungry anticipation, the minutes seemed to crawl by. To Timmy, eagerly awaiting vindication, they went scarcely faster. But to Fletch, they fairly flew, impervious to his efforts to detain them.

Even so, he was startled when Injun got to his feet, head cocked toward the stairs. Good God! Gann couldn't be coming back already, could he? He could; Injun called, "Hey, Pappy—that you?" and got an answering murmur of acknowledgment.

"Thank goodness!" Timmy declared with such satisfaction that he felt an irrational anger at her heartlessness. Yet she couldn't know that Gann's return spelled tragedy, not triumph. He fixed his eyes dumbly on the stairwell and waited for his judges.

Lionel Gann came lightly down the steps, followed by Blossom with the others close behind. Their expressions were indiscernible in the shadows.

"Well?" Injun asked eagerly. "What happened?"

Gann held out his hand. "Give me your knife."

"Hey, don't scab me," Injun protested, disappointed at being deprived of his reward. "You promised, Pappy." Gann snapped his fingers impatiently and Injun surrendered the weapon with a scowl.

It was all over; the verdict was in, the sentence pronounced. He was going to die here, his jugular severed or his belly sundered, as helpless to prevent it as a trussed chicken. As Gann came toward him, knife poised, he opened his mouth to say something, anything, that would delay the execution . . . and discovered his throat too constricted to speak. Only a muffled squawk emerged.

Gann didn't appear to notice. Timmy flung herself in his way; he thrust her aside. With one brisk slash, he cut the rope which tethered Fletch to the ceiling. A second slash freed his wrists. So unexpected was it that he continued to sit on the apple box, unable to move and still halfway expecting that his body would be the knife's next target. When Gann thrust out his hand, he flinched until he realized that the hand was now empty.

"I owe you an apology," Gann said, his voice seeming to come from a great distance off. "All you left of COIN was small change."

Then the others were clustering around him also, each adding excited details. Fletch scarcely heard them nor was he more than dimly aware that Timmy was hugging him fiercely.

"You all right?" Gann inquired, puzzled by his catatonic behavior. "I thought you'd be plenty happy to hear the good news."

Fletch struggled to regain his composure and his voice and found them both, nearly as good as new. "What the hell," he said with a shrug. "I never had any doubt about it."

# Eleven

THE TOOL BOX BOMB had performed better than anyone expected, Fletch learned, due to an unforeseen accident which could be considered either lucky or unlucky, depending on the point of view. The blast had ignited a gas line in the adjacent wall and the timbers of the seventy-five-year-old mansion had proved highly combustible fuel. Engine companies had been summoned from as far away as Tarzana to the west and Glendale to the east. According to the latest news bulletin, the blaze was now contained. The basement and main floor were reported gutted with damage estimated at over half a million dollars.

Official statements placed the blame on "radical elements," promised an unrelenting search for the culprits and expressed thankfulness that no lives had been lost. An unidentified spokesman for COIN—presumably General Sugarman—downplayed the attack, claiming it would not hinder his organization's work in the slightest, while vowing grimly in the next breath that steps were being taken to prevent any repetition of the outrage.

Fletch was at a loss to understand how it had happened at all. Why had General Sugarman, warned in advance, permitted the bomb to explode? It seemed inconceivable that he would forget to alert the police or that they would ignore the summons. Yet two facts were plain: COIN lay shattered and smoldering . . . and he, the make-believe outlaw, was now the genuine article.

But these reflections came later. At the moment, he could only give silent thanks to whatever gods had intervened to spare him. The mansion could be restored; his life could not.

When all the witnesses to the bombing had given their own versions of it, not once but several times, and when the excitement in the cellar commenced to subside, Gann called a halt to the celebration. "I think it's time we had a serious talk, Fletch, just the two of us."

"Your place or mine?"

"Better make it yours."

"Can't it wait?" Timmy protested, hovering over Fletch like a concerned mother hen. "Just look at him, Pappy. He's still shook from what Injun did to him while you were gone."

"What Injun did to him," Gann repeated. He shot an ominous glance at his hatchet man. "Tell me more. I'd like to hear how my orders were obeyed."

She was only too willing to oblige but Fletch cut her off. "What happened is between Injun and me, nobody else."

Gann studied him for a moment before he shrugged. "All right, I'll keep my hands off this time, if that's the way you want it. But if it ever happens again . . ."

Injun reprieved was not Injun thankful; he interpreted mercy as weakness. "It wasn't nothing to bark about, anyhow." He held out his hand. "I'll take my knife back now."

"Allow me," Fletch said, plucking the weapon from Gann's grasp. "I'd like the pleasure of returning it."

There was a sudden chill silence in the cellar save for the television where two improbable housewives were bickering over the merits of their respective detergents. Gann said quickly, "Now hold on, Fletch—"

"You promised to keep your hands off," Fletch reminded him. Three paces separated him from his enemy.

He closed the gap to one, the knife pointed at its owner's naked and suddenly quivering stomach.

"Pappy?" Injun whispered. "You ain't gonna let him . . ."

The cry for help went unanswered. Injun's eyes darted from face to face, seeking an ally and finding none, then fell to the razor-sharp blade. A whimper escaped his lips. "Who's sweating now?" Fletch asked softly. With the sure timing of the professional actor, he let the silence continue and the tension build, then broke both with a chuckle. He reversed the knife in his hand and thrust the butt toward the other man.

A universal sigh of relief, almost a moan, was wrenched from the others. Only Injun himself seemed unable to believe that he had been spared. He continued to hold his paralyzed stance, mute and unmoving.

"Go ahead," Fletch invited. "Take it."

This time Injun believed. His eyes rose slowly from the knife to the author of his humiliation and in them lay a sly and savage resolve. As he reached for the weapon, Fletch kicked him in the genitals. So vicious was the blow and so solid the impact that he feared for an instant that he had broken a toe. Yet the pain he felt was small in comparison to that which he inflicted. Injun's mouth flew open. From it came a high-pitched scream. He fell to the cellar floor, writhing there like a wounded snake, while his hands pressed against his groin in a vain effort to ease its agony.

The remaining guerrillas gazed down upon their stricken comrade with expressions which ranged from shock to satisfaction. No one appeared to question the justness of the punishment or Fletch's right to administer it. Choogle delivered the collective judgment. "I guess he got what he deserved."

They considered the account settled. Fletch did not. The kick was for me, he told Injun silently. You still haven't paid for Curt. Aloud, he said, "You mentioned a talk,

Pappy. Let's have at it."

As they climbed the stairs to the second floor, Gann said thoughtfully, "You had me hyped completely, Fletch. I was watching your eyes and I swear I thought you meant to gut him."

"You sorry I didn't?"

"No. I hope you won't be, either. Injun's never going to forgive you."

Wrong, Fletch thought; it's *us* he's not going to forgive. Long after the pain had vanished, Injun would remember that Gann, the master he served, had been willing to see him humbled, even killed. He would certainly try to pay back Fletch but, equally certain, he would try to pay back Gann as well—and in this, Fletch intended to give him all possible assistance. Slowly but surely, he was isolating Gann from his followers, setting one against the other. When the showdown finally arrived, there would be no need for him to play their executioner. They themselves would do that job for him.

So he replied with complete honesty, "I figured Injun was more use alive than dead. Now it's up to you to convince him the same goes for me." He opened the door to the room he shared with Timmy and lit the candle to dispel the darkness. "Sorry I can't offer you a chair but they haven't delivered our furniture yet."

Gann took his customary cross-legged position on the floor. The guerrilla leader appeared at an uncharacteristic loss for words. Finally he said, "I've been trying to think how to say this. It isn't easy so bear with me. Call it a confession if you like. Tonight made me realize something that's going to take some getting used to."

Fletch waited, wondering what this strange introduction was leading up to. Gann continued, "When the bomb went off, I found I was actually disappointed. I was hoping you'd fail. All along I'd told myself that it was the security of the tribe that concerned me—when really it was my

106

own security I was worried about. I saw you as a threat to my leadership."

Fletch was less surprised by the admission—since it revealed nothing he didn't already know—than by Gann's willingness to make it. Though spurning conventional morality, Gann had his own twisted code in which murder was permissible but ego was not. "Let it slide," Fletch told him. "All you're saying is that you're human."

"That's not good enough. A leader must be superior to those he leads. I've proved I'm not. So I'm stepping down, Fletch. You're the PTA's new leader."

For just an instant, he was tempted to accept if only because the irony appealed to him. But while taking command of the enemy would constitute a truly magnificent con, he doubted his ability to carry off the role. His rebel veneer was painfully thin; it could not withstand the close and constant scrutiny a leader must endure. Furthermore, he was not entirely convinced of Gann's sincerity. The grotesque proposal might well be a trap. And so he shook his head. "You're still the best man for the job and we both know it. I've tried to make it clear from the beginning that I don't have eyes to be numero uno. If there's been a problem between us, it's because you didn't believe me. I hope you will now."

He was not the only one to wonder if the offer was genuine. "Damn," Gann said softly. "Now I'll never be sure whether I meant it or not. I'd like to believe I did—but I'll admit I'm not sorry you turned it down. Thanks for the vote of confidence, Fletch. I'll try to be worthy of it."

"You lead, I'll follow. All I ask is to know where we're going."

"You certainly deserve that. Just let me clear it with the Co-op and . . ." He broke off and slammed his fist on the floor. "No, damn it! The least I can do is give you the broad outline. Did you see this evening's headlines?"

"No. I was busy making tomorrow's."

"Bruno's trial is over. The case went to the jury at noon. I expect they'll bring back a verdict within twenty-four hours, forty-eight at the outside. No need to ask what that verdict's going to be. Or the sentence, either."

"Just between us—is Bruno really guilty?"

"Are you kidding? That's beside the point. The Toppies would put Bruno away for life even if he wasn't. They figure they'll scare the hell out of the rest of us naughty boys and girls. The D.A.'s practically said as much."

Fletch yawned. "So what else is new?"

"We're confronted with two choices. The first is to let nature take its course and exploit Bruno as a martyr, as you suggested a couple of nights back. But we've already got enough martyrs. We don't need another. We do need Bruno. He's the one man in the party who can unify all the various factions. Without him, we're fragmented."

"Maybe if you asked them real nice, the Toppies would turn him loose."

"That's our second choice," Gann agreed with complete seriousness. "Except that we're not going to ask them. We're going to tell them. They've got our leader. We'll take one of theirs. Whether they get him back alive or dead depends on them."

"You know which the Toppies will have to choose, don't you?"

"No, I don't—and neither do you. It's a changing world, Fletch, the old guidelines don't apply. Sure, the Toppies boast that they'll never bargain at the point of a gun. But they said the same thing in Vietnam, too. They're weak. When the chips are down, they fold, more often than not. We're willing to die for what we believe. Are they? They haven't proved it yet. What it boils down to is this: Whose commitment is the greater?"

What it really boiled down to, Fletch thought, was kidnapping and murder. Like most fanatics, Gann was incapable of understanding the adversary's psychology. What he saw as the society's weakness—the ability, however reluctantly employed, to accept reasonable compromise—was actually its strength. But what Gann and his urban guerrillas proposed was neither reasonable nor compromise. It was a demand to commit suicide and the society must inevitably reject it. Since this opinion would constitute heresy in Gann's eyes, he kept it to himself. "Suppose the Toppies do agree to deal for Bruno—where do we go from there?"

"We fly Bruno out of the country. I can't tell you where but it's all been arranged. He announces the formation of a government-in-exile and proclaims a war of national liberation, a new American Revolution. We'll present our case to the world, maybe even take it to the UN . . . while simultaneously mounting an all-out offensive here at home." Gann's face was rapt as, in imagination, he saw a government crumble and another rise to take its place. Then he sighed. "But, like I said, it all depends on our freeing Bruno."

"I see what you mean. Okay, who gets snatched and when?"

"Sorry, Fletch. That's top-level secret. I will tell you who's going to do the snatching, though. Us. The PTA has been designated as the primary strike force for Operation Mother."

"Operation Mother!" Fletch echoed with a laugh. "You've got to be kidding."

"You'll understand the significance when the time comes," Gann promised. "For the moment, you're to keep what I've told you in strictest confidence. Don't let on to the others that you know any more than they do." He prepared to rise, then paused. "Oh, one more thing. If it should prove necessary to execute our hostage, I want it done in a way that will wring the last drop of horror from it. You might start thinking about that. Your handling of the COIN caper proves you have a flair for the dramatic."

"I'll give it my best shot," Fletch agreed as nonchalantly as if they were discussing a routine business venture rather than the cold-blooded slaying of a fellow human being. "How much time do I have?"

"A few days, at least. We won't make our move until Bruno's been sentenced." This time he got to his feet. "Going to join us below—or do you still prefer to camp here?"

"Here, I guess. Timmy doesn't dig an audience. Me, I could care less."

"What is she to you, anyway?" Gann asked curiously. "Aside from the obvious, I mean."

"Isn't that enough?"

"Well, since it's nothing serious . . ." He hesitated. "It might be better for all concerned if you gave her to Injun. That'd help restore harmony and keep you a free agent. And if you've just got to swive somebody, try Blossom or Midge. Or both."

Fletch promised that he would consider it. And promptly forgot about it. Later, however, he remembered and, as he and Timmy prepared for sleep, repeated the suggestion for her amusement. Her reaction surprised him. "Are you going to do it?" she asked.

"Hell, no! What kind of stupid question is that?"

"Maybe you should. Injun wants me—and you don't."

"How'd you arrive at that conclusion?"

"You said this afternoon that you were only waiting for me to give you the green light. Well, I've given it to you and what have you done about it? Nothing, that's what." She held up a hand to forestall a denial. "I thought for a while tonight—when you warned Injun you'd total him if he touched me—that you loved me like I love you. But that was just an act, wasn't it? That's all it's ever been."

"That isn't true, Timmy."

"If it isn't," she said quietly, "then why am I over here and you're over there?"

There was only one convincing answer to that and it did not involve words. Yet, for a reason he could not comprehend, he drew back from making it; some instinct warned that he would regret it. And then he thought, don't be a damn fool. You wanted revenge, didn't you? To a woman, rape was the ultimate humiliation; not without reason had it once been called the fate worse than death.

He meant to violate her, to use her body with contempt as victorious warriors have traditionally used the enemy's women. But he discovered he could not. As their flesh fused, as they strained together, rushing as one with an excitement almost too great to endure toward a conclusion indescribably sweet, he knew the truth. Sugarman had warned him not to hate Timmy and he had obeyed. But no one had warned him not to fall in love with her.

# Twelve

"WHAT ARE YOU THINKING?" Timmy whispered.

"About you, naturally." It was not merely a lover's reassurance. The woman who lay pleasantly exhausted in his arms was indeed the focus of his thoughts, although not for the reason she supposed.

"Me, too. You were so strong . . ."

"Did I hurt you?"

"Just a little, in the beginning. But I didn't mind—it was all too fantastic. Better than it's ever been. I never really expected it could be this way."

"Neither did I."

Again she assumed they meant the same thing and snuggled closer. "Don't ever leave me," she murmured drowsily. "I'd die if you did. You're my everything."

He lay awake long after she had fallen asleep. What in God's name am I going to do? he wondered. He had vowed to punish his brother's murderers, Timmy among them. He still hungered for vengeance but Timmy had awakened in him a new hunger, equally fierce. Yet he could not satisfy both; the two were mutually exclusive. He tried to convince himself that he was mistaking lust for love, and failed. Lust he had known before, and frequently. Compared to this present feeling, it was a single violin against a full orchestra. He did not want merely her body; he wanted her. He tried to construct a compromise between conscience and desire, and again he failed. Grim reality held him like a vise. Timmy was guilty. Timmy must pay. But even after he had bowed to this stern judgment, one half of his mind still cunningly sought to bargain. What if Timmy were not really guilty, after all— or, if guilty, not as guilty as the others? Why not give her the benefit of the doubt? There is no doubt, scoffed the other half. Furthermore, he could not live with doubt, much less love with it. And, at last, he found the only possible solution to his dilemma. He could not force himself to condemn Timmy. He must force her to condemn herself.

Since a blunt demand for the truth would not serve, he began his search for it the next morning by inviting Timmy in a teasing fashion to compare him with her previous lovers.

"You jealous?" she asked hopefully. "Well, don't be, darling. There's only been one other—Ken—and now that I've found you . . ."

"How about that other guy, the one you said could almost be my brother? Curt somebody."

Timmy looked surprised. "Oh, there was nothing like that with him!"

"I got the impression you rather grooved on him."

"Well, I did—in a way. And maybe if things had worked out different—"

"What things, Timmy?"

"I told you what happened to him, didn't I?"

"You told me he died. You didn't tell me how or why."

"It was a real bad scene." Timmy shuddered. "Curt got hit by a train."

"Accident, you mean?"

"No," she said slowly, "it wasn't an accident. It was just made to look like one."

His last feeble spark of hope perished. Timmy could not know that Curt had been murdered without being implicated in it. He asked the final, now unnecessary question. "Who would do a thing like that?"

Her answer stunned him. "The pigs, who else?"

He begged her to repeat and, even when she had done so, still was not sure he understood. "Are you saying that the cops stuck him in front of a train? Why, for God's sake?"

"To get rid of him, natch. Vince—I mean Curt—was a big man in the movement back East. The Toppies had been trying to put him down for a long time. The way Pappy figures, they saw a chance to zap him permanently and they took it."

Timmy obviously believed the bizarre theory. For just an instant Fletch himself wondered. He had no actual proof to the contrary, only Sugarman's unsupported word . . . But he knew better, proof or no proof. Curt had been Gann's enemy, not Sugarman's. Gann, not Sugarman, had put him to death. Gann was guilty—but of even greater importance, Timmy was not. Gann, for reasons of his own, had chosen to keep her in ignorance. Which explained, at last, her presence at Curt's funeral: sorrow for a friend rather than triumph over a foe. "I love you," he told her and, for the first time, could make the statement without reservation.

But while one burden was lifted, he immediately felt the weight of another. He must contrive to lead Gann and his fellow outlaws to slaughter while somehow seeing to it that Timmy escaped the shambles. And—to make a difficult job more difficult still—without her realizing either his aim or his motivation. Timmy loved Chris Fletcher, the supposed guerrilla. He could not be at all certain she would feel the same about Fletcher Orr, the enemy agent.

He decided to test the waters with a tentative toe. "You happy here with me, Timmy?"

"Happy? That doesn't even begin to say it."

"Think you could be just as happy with me someplace else? Suppose I decided all of a sudden to split this scene

—what would you do?"

Her eyebrows lifted with surprise. "I'd split with you, dummy. You ought to know that by now."

"You mean you'd be willing to give up all this just for me?"

"Say the word and I'll start packing." She grinned, secure in the belief that he had no such intention. "But now that you mention it, I would miss our room. It's, well, like home, you know? I was thinking that I might fix it up a little, maybe make some curtains . . ."

Fletch was encouraged by her reaction. He longed to reveal the whole truth but dared not. The charade was far from over. His debt to the dead aside, he had a responsibility to the living, not only Timmy but also the person code-named Mother. He debated alerting Sugarman to the plot and reluctantly decided that it would be premature. He could predict Sugarman's response: Learn Mother's identity at all costs. Until they knew whom the guerrillas planned to kidnap, there was little they could do to prevent it. He must wait, not by choice but by necessity, for Gann to give him that information. Then, and only then, could he arrange the ambush which—he devoutly hoped—would end not only Gann's life but his dream as well.

At four o'clock that afternoon, Bruno Sledge's jury set Operation Mother into operation by finding the defendant guilty on three counts of first-degree murder and two counts of aggravated assault. Sledge was exonerated of a sixth charge, conspiracy, but that scarcely mattered. The jury was instructed to return the following day to hear arguments regarding the punishment which, under California law, they rather than the judge would determine.

Fletch attended the penalty phase at Gann's invitation. The courtroom was considerably less crowded than during the trial itself. The verdict had ended the show as far as most of the public was concerned; the rest was anticlimactic. Fletch, however, knew that what they considered the end was in reality the beginning of an even grimmer drama. He viewed Bruno Sledge with fascination and was a trifle surprised at what he saw. Although his position was virtually hopeless, the guerrillas' prime minister exhibited a steely self-confidence that surpassed mere bravado. During his trial, he had taken the attitude that society, not he, was in the dock. Sledge continued to proclaim that belief, disrupting proceedings with obscene tirades against his enemies and threatening them with retribution, until the judge ordered him removed from the courtroom.

With the star gone, Fletch studied the supporting players: the flamboyant and politically ambitious district attorney, the harried and soon-to-retire judge, the anonymous and exhausted jurors. Was one of these the person dubbed Mother?

Gann declined to commit himself. "Hell, they're all mothers," he said, using the term in the manner of the underground, as an epithet. "But I can think of lots of others. Can't you?"

Fletch tried. He began to watch the television news programs faithfully, seeking to select from among the many prominent names and familiar faces the one the guerrilla coalition might consider most suitable as their hostage. Though reason argued that it must be a man, he could not rule out women. Gann had told him that the code name had been chosen for its aptness. The list of potential candidates grew longer by the hour—and included both the newly crowned Mrs. America, a resident of nearby Gardena, and the Vice-President of the United States who was scheduled to attend a fund-raising dinner in Los Angeles the following week. The former seemed ludicrous and the latter, in view of the tight security which enveloped the nation's second highest elected official, unlikely. But even with these two subtracted, an appallingly large number of possibilities remained.

The penalty phase of the Sledge trial began on Tuesday. Gann predicted that it would all be over by Friday since the weary jurors did not relish the prospect of spending yet another weekend separated from their families. Gann proved an excellent prophet. The jury received the case at eleven o'clock Friday morning. Six hours and three ballots later, Bruno Sledge stood condemned to life imprisonment without possibility of parole. The judge ordered him returned for formal sentencing the following Monday. The trial had been one of the most lengthy in the history of California; now the state apparently intended to make up for lost time.

Some of the PTA were dismayed by the speedy progression of events. Not Lionel Gann. "I've been waiting months for this moment," he told Fletch jubilantly. "Now we can stop talking and start swinging. The Co-op's meeting tonight to settle the final details. I want you there with me."

Fletch concealed his own jubilation. During the past week, he had come to fear that Gann might choose to keep the name of the prospective hostage secret until the last possible moment, leaving Fletch no time to take countermeasures. His fear had been groundless. Before the night was over, he would know all there was to know about Operation Mother—including how to defeat it.

He managed to steal a moment alone with Timmy. "Remember what I told you the other day? We're in for a kinky time. So keep your scope out—and if I decide to hat it up in a tearing hurry, don't give me any static, okay?"

"How come you're so yancy?" she asked, worried by his grim tone. "Are you in some sort of trouble?"

"Could be. I'll let you know definitely when I get back."

She held on to his hands, reluctant to let him go. "You are coming back, aren't you?"

"I'll come back for you, Timmy. That's a promise."

The Co-op, Fletch learned as they drove to the meeting, had no permanent headquarters and seldom used the same rendezvous twice. Vastly outnumbered and facing a foe armed with monitoring devices of incredible sophistication, the guerrillas' defense lay in their mobility. That, and a thorough suspicion of everyone—including each other. Gann admitted as much. "Bringing you along is sure going to tear up some of the brethren. I'm laying myself wide open to a lot of brutal criticism. But, what the hell, you'll be running the strike force in case anything should happen to me and you've got to have the whole picture."

"I thought I already had the whole picture—except Mother's real name."

Gann refused to take the bait. "All I've given you so far is the overall strategy. What you'll hear tonight is the nitty and the gritty, not just about Operation Mother but the Co-op's fall-back plans in case Operation Mother gets snuffed."

"I guess there's always that possibility."

"I'd say the odds are about sixty-forty that the Toppies won't agree to swap hostages. In that case, we up the ante. If they won't deal for one life, how about a hundred lives —or a thousand?"

"You thinking of bombing a plane?"

"That's been suggested. Personally, I prefer something more imaginative. Are you aware that the Army has been quietly transferring its stockpile of chemical and biological weapons from Utah to an island in the Pacific? Two shipments passed through the port of Los Angeles within the last month. There'll be more. What if one of them had an accident?"

"Oh, the people here are so used to the smog they probably wouldn't even notice." Yet he was far from taking the threat lightly. Gann and his confederates were quite capable of carrying it out—or others equally horrible. And, incredible though it seemed, without even considering them to be horrible. The guerrilla chieftains were victims of the monomania characteristic of all political movements which have as their goal the total regeneration of mankind. To those who nourish a vision of universal utopia, ordinary morality becomes merely a hangup to be scorned. Never mind that they must inevitably perish, victims of their own poison. Unfortunately, the structure of modern society was so complex, and by this complexity so vulnerable to attack, that a good many innocent persons might perish with them. More than ever, he realized the absolute necessity of stopping them now, not only to save their first hostage but all the hostages yet to come.

"Here we are," Gann said, interrupting his train of thought. "Park anywhere in this block."

For tonight's meeting, the Co-op had chosen a small office building on Figueroa Boulevard. The graceless architecture had never aspired to beauty even in its youth. With the coming of middle age, the three-story concrete structure was no longer functional, either. Like the dreary neighborhood in which it stood, it offered nothing to attract the newcomer or inducement to persuade old-timers to stay. The "Offices for Rent or Lease" sign was nearly as old as the building itself. However, there remained enough of an aura of shabby respectability to provide adequate camouflage for the outlaws.

Gann directed him to remain with the bus. "I can't take you inside without the Co-op's okay. Sit tight and I'll come back for you just as soon as they give it."

Fletch sat. Traffic on the boulevard was light and on the sidewalk almost nonexistent. The small shops and businesses had long since closed their doors save for the liquor store in the middle of the next block. A police sedan cruised by, slowing briefly to allow its occupants to scrutinize him, then continued its patrol. He felt no apprehension that his presence might arouse the law's suspicion. Los Angeles, with far more automobiles than garages in which to house them, used its streets as an all-night parking lot.

Waiting to be summoned, he let his thoughts leap past the next few hours to those which lay beyond it. The terrorists did not plan to put Operation Mother into effect until Bruno Sledge had been formally sentenced. That gave him the weekend, two full days. Tomorrow he would contact Sugarman, place the entire blueprint for Operation Mother (and perhaps even more) in his hands and let the general take it from there, leaving for himself the responsibility of seeing that Timmy . . .

A harsh voice, only a foot or so from his left ear, caused him to jump. "Don't make any sudden moves," it warned. "Keep your hands on the wheel where I can see them. Police officers."

Startled, Fletch turned his head to look at the man who had materialized so surprisingly beside the open window. The glare of a flashlight at point-blank range blinded him, making visual identification impossible. However, the voice alone was enough. The flat guttural tones belonged to Sergeant Ike Quinsler—disparagingly dubbed IQ— the cop he had mistakenly assaulted on Timmy's behalf . . . and whom he had, until this moment, nearly forgotten.

# Thirteen

HE MIGHT HAVE FORGOTTEN Quinsler, but IQ had not forgotten him. "It's him, all right," he announced. Fletch realized that Quinsler had a partner. As his eyes adjusted to the glare, he saw that the partner was a lanky plainclothes detective and that he held a pistol pointed at Fletch's head. Quinsler flung open the car door. "Out," he invited. "Nice and slow." He followed the order with a shove which sent Fletch into an unbalanced leaning position against the automobile's side. Quinsler ran his hands expertly over his body to satisfy himself that his captive carried no weapon. "Okay. You can turn around."

Fletch opened his mouth to attempt some explanation, however feeble, which might rescue him from this potential calamity. A fist in the pit of his stomach drove the breath from his lungs. He doubled over, gasping, and was knocked to the pavement by a second blow across the back of his neck.

"Hey, look at that, Sol," Quinsler exclaimed with mock surprise. "The creep fell down."

"Yeah," the detective called Sol replied. "Seems like he did, at that."

"Hurt yourself?" IQ bent to assist Fletch to rise, then sent him sprawling with a knee to the chin. "The creep can't stand up," he complained. "Wouldn't be surprised if he's stoned to the eyes. Acid maybe, or H. What do you think, Sol?"

"Lot of that going around," Sol agreed dispassionately. Again Quinsler offered his hand. Fletch tried to scramble away to avoid more punishment. The result was the same; this time his kidneys were the target. "Resisting arrest, huh?" IQ crowed. He forced Fletch's arms behind his back and confined them there with handcuffs. He jerked the by now thoroughly helpless prisoner to his feet. The beating he had administered seemed to inflame his anger rather than assuage it, as if nothing less than death would constitute a proper vengeance.

The other detective appeared to sense it also. "Take it easy, Ike," he advised. "Any more and you're gonna catch hell from the board for sure."

Quinsler shook off his partner's hand. "I am taking it easy. He's still breathing, ain't he?" Nevertheless, the warning carried weight. "Okay, Officer, better put the suspect in the car before he falls down again."

Fletch was half-marched, half-carried to the police sedan which waited around the corner. He was deposited in the rear seat. He sprawled there, fighting waves of nausea which threatened to engulf him. Blood was running down his face but he could not wipe it away or stanch the flow with his hands shackled behind him. Reason told him it would be useless to ask for assistance.

While his partner started the engine, Quinsler used the radio to notify central police headquarters of the situation. "KMA, this is Special Unit One Niner Three. Report a possible Four-eleven in custody. We are abandoning loop surveillance Area Charlie Victor and are en route precinct."

"Roger, One Nine Three," the dispatcher replied. "We log you Code Six. Advise on your return to station."

They drove on in silence. Quinsler broke it with a chuckle. "God, when I think how I damn near let my hemorrhoids talk me out of pulling the duty tonight! Something told me to stick with it. If I hadn't, I might never have caught up with the bastard."

"You absolutely sure it's him, Ike?"

"I never forget a man who busts me in the mouth. Besides, there's that red bus. Half a dozen people saw him drive away in it, him and the girl. Jesus! I wonder if that's who the creep was waiting for? Maybe we ought to swing back for a look-see, just in case."

"Time to think of that was before you logged out," Sol objected. "Go back now and they'll have us filling out Form Twenty Dash Ones till we're blue in the face."

"Yeah, damn it. Oh well, mustn't be greedy. By the way, Sol, don't let me forget to send a truck to pick up the creep's car. Wouldn't surprise me if it turns out to be hot."

Fletch wriggled his way closer to the steel mesh which separated him from the two officers. "If you'll just listen to me a minute—"

"We will, we will," Quinsler purred. "We're the best goddam listeners in the world—right, Sol? But you listen to me first, creep." He cleared his throat. "I wish to inform you of your constitutional right to remain silent and of your right to legal counsel. You are not compelled to answer any questions or to make any statement. Should you choose to do so of your own free will, without duress or coercion or promise of immunity thereby, such statement or statements may be entered into evidence against you. That clear? Good. Wouldn't want some shyster to louse up an open-and-shut case now, would we?"

"Give me a break," Fletch implored. "I admit I slugged you but it was all a mistake. I thought you were someone else. Anyway, you've already paid me back in spades. Isn't that enough?"

Quinsler ignored him. "Interfering with a police officer in the pursuit of his duties, assault with intent to do great bodily harm, leaving the scene of a felony, resisting arrest . . . I like it, I like it. And when you throw in the possibles—possession and use of dangerous drugs, vagrancy, grand theft auto—what does that add up to, Sol? Ten-to-twenty, at least."

"Who you kidding?" Sol replied with more than a tinge of bitterness. "Courts these days are on his side, not ours, and you damn well know it. Mark my words, he'll cop a plea and wind up doing six months in County, maybe less."

The prediction did not cheer Fletch any more than it did Quinsler. Six months or six years, either spelled disaster; he could not spare even six hours. With him neutralized—and, ironically, not by his enemies but by his allies—there was nothing and no one to prevent the terrorists from carrying out Operation Mother with fatal results to all concerned. He must convince the police to release him before it was too late. Since Ike Quinsler would not listen to reason, his only hope lay in finding someone who would.

The admitting officer at the precinct house was not that someone. He took charge of the prisoner with the bored air of a man operating an assembly line. His job was to process the raw material and pass it on. He had long since ceased to regard the never-ending flow as human beings like himself or to listen to their protests. Fletch was booked, fingerprinted and photographed. His few personal belongings were removed and sealed in a brown envelope. His demands to speak with someone in authority were ignored; when he persisted, he was advised to shut up if he knew what was good for him. Another officer, equally indifferent, marched him to a holding cell.

The holding cell—commonly called "the tank"—was a large windowless room without furniture. About two dozen other men sat, sprawled or slept on the steel benches which rimmed it. Another dozen lay on the concrete floor, too stupefied by alcohol or drugs to care. The stench was oppressive and the air was stifling, but nobody seemed to care about that either.

Fletch stayed by the grilled door, hoping to hail some-one who might prove a friend. One of his fellow prisoners, a grizzled wino known as Bones, advised him out of long experience that there was no use making a fuss, sonny. "They'll get around to you when they're damn good and ready, not a minute before." And how soon did Bones esti-mate that to be? An hour, a day, a week; one guess was as good as another. Fletch's refusal to accept his fate philo-sophically evoked a derisive cackle in which some of the other men joined.

Yet his defiance appeared to be justified when, after an hour or so (it was impossible to tell time without a clock), the officer who had brought him to the tank appeared to summon him from it. He learned shortly that he was not being set free. Instead, manacled once more, he was driven downtown to the main jail, known to the underground as "the glasshouse" by virtue of its myriad windows. There he again went through the routine of being admitted. Al-though the procedure was the same, methodical and imper-sonal, his new jailers were a shade more communicative than the old. One even bothered to ask what had happened to his face—then answered his own question. "Must have fallen down, right?"

Fletch saw no advantage in contradicting him. "Ser-geant, I've got to talk to whoever's in charge. It's a matter of life and death."

The officer was unimpressed. "Forget it, fella." How-ever, Fletch might use the pay telephone to notify his fam-ily, contact his attorney or attempt to raise bail. The offi-cer felt that the last would be a waste of time and a dime. Bondsmen took a dim view of felony suspects without identification or financial resources and Fletch lacked both.

"I've got somebody who'll vouch for me." He dialed the number at which Sugarman had promised he might be reached around the clock. To his chagrin, there was no an-swer.

"Tough," the officer told him with a yawn. "Looks like you'll be with us for the weekend, don't it?"

"That's impossible!"

"Wanna bet?" Since the following day was Saturday, court would not convene again until Monday morning. Neither, the officer guessed, would Fletch be able to secure the services of an attorney before then. Lawyers, like doctors, were usually unavailable during the weekend—and particularly so to new clients. The public defender? "He's a lawyer too, ain't he? You won't see him around here before Monday either."

Fletch was led through a succession of steel gates—he counted seven in all between himself and freedom—to cell block B. Here the officer in charge filled out a card for the new arrival and put it into a large rack containing a number of similar cards. Another gate, the eighth, admitted him to a narrow hallway called "the freeway" that bisected two identical rows of cells. A ninth gate, operated by remote control, opened on cell B-3.

B-3, like each of its fellows, contained three sets of steel double bunks. All six beds were occupied. Fletch was forced to make do with a mattress on the floor and a single blanket, both filthy.

He was suddenly furious at both fate and its callous instruments. He kicked the mattress but only succeeded in hurting his toe; his shoes had been removed on orders of his jailers. Rattling the bars of his cage and yelling for the guard proved no more productive. His cellmates commanded him profanely to go to sleep and let them do likewise. Fletch finally surrendered. He was stuck here for tonight and there was not a damn thing he could do about it. But just wait, he vowed. As soon as morning comes . . .

Morning came quickly. Reveille was at 5 A.M. and was announced by a blaring loudspeaker. Fletch was the only one to heed it. His fellow prisoners, more experienced in the routine, did not rise for another twenty minutes, at which time the remote-controlled door slid open briefly. Upon that signal, they erupted from their bunks and hastened to form a line in the freeway together with their neighbors from adjoining cells. Another quarter hour passed before the guard appeared to march them to breakfast.

The meal, served cafeteria-style from steam tables manned by trusties, consisted of two overfried eggs, underdone potatoes, hot cakes which looked like cardboard and had as little taste, and lukewarm coffee. The prisoners were allowed ten minutes to eat, which in Fletch's case was more than ample time, before they were returned to their cells. Most of the men thereupon went back to sleep until the loudspeaker again roused them at eight by calling out the names of those to be released or to go on sick call or to confer with the chaplain.

Fletch was not included in the list. However, he fell out in the freeway with the chosen few, hoping not to escape but only to gain an audience with higher authority. The ruse was detected immediately. In vain he pleaded a need for, first, medical and, that failing, spiritual attention—and was refused both on the grounds that such requests must be made twenty-four hours in advance.

"I have to see somebody! I've got important information to give you. Won't you please tell whoever's in charge here that I want to talk to him?"

"Sure, fella, anything you say," the cell block commander assured him. "Now suppose you move back where you belong while I'm getting hold of the captain."

Fletch returned to B-3, somewhat encouraged. The six men who shared it with him were quick to dash his hopes. "What kinda trip you on, man, mouthing off that way? You're just gonna press The Man's buttons, that's all. Ain't nobody here gonna do you no favors, dig? The captain see you? No way. You could bleed to death and The Deacon wouldn't even give you a Band-Aid."

They were well equipped to be his teachers; he was the only one to whom jail was a new experience. And the only Caucasian. Of the other men, three were black, one was Korean and two Mexican. Their offenses ranged from drug peddling and wife-beating to car theft and attempted rape. Only one had been sentenced for his crime. The others, unable to raise bail, were serving "dead time" ranging from two days to two weeks while awaiting trial.

Although set apart from them by color, culture and experience, Fletch was treated with amused condescension rather than hostility. He was, in fact, welcomed— initially because he might have cigarettes (which sold on the jail black market at more than a dollar per pack); then, that hope dashed, because he provided fresh fuel for conversation. B-3 was twelve feet wide by sixteen feet long. Most of the space was taken up by the bunks, the commode and the wash basin. Since there was little room in which to move about, the prisoners were compelled to remain in their bunks. With no books to read, television to watch or view to admire, they were compelled to pass the time talking. Mostly, they talked about themselves, the misfortunes (never merited) which had led them to jail and the precautions (ever foolproof) that would prevent their return. Called upon for his own autobiography, Fletch was as mendacious as any. To reveal the truth would cause his cellmates to brand him a police spy— they could hardly be expected to comprehend the difference between a COIN agent and a conventional police officer—and thus invite the treatment usually dealt out to informers. His real history would have to wait for a more appreciative audience.

In the middle of the morning, a trusty came by selling newspapers . . . but though Fletch watched the freeway anxiously, no one else appeared. When they fell out at eleven o'clock for lunch, he asked the cell block commander if the captain had received his message. "Knock it off, will you?" the officer advised him. "I've had just about enough of your crap so move along, you're holding up the line."

Fletch moved along, to the accompaniment of sotto voce I-told-you-sos from his cell mates. He offered no defense; it was now obvious that they were right and that further pleading was useless. Okay, he thought grimly, if I can't get what I want by being nice, maybe I can get it by being naughty.

Lunch amounted to boiled ham, sliced so thin it was nearly transparent, potatoes left over from breakfast, canned peas and a watery pudding. The trusty who served him interpreted his expression correctly. "Don't blame me, man. I just dish it out. Ain't nothing in the rules says you gotta eat it."

"What do the rules say about this?" He hurled the tray and its unappetizing contents at the nearest wall.

He expected to cause a commotion; he did not expect to trigger a riot. Several of the other prisoners, as displeased with the menu as he but until now unwilling to do more than grumble about it, took inspiration from his example. The mess hall erupted in a bedlam of shouts, curses and the clanging of steel trays against concrete. Fletch found himself the unwitting leader of a small mutiny.

It lasted no more than a minute. The guards charged the mutineers, pacifiers swinging, and rapidly restored order. "Who started it?" the cell block commander demanded. When told, he glared at Fletch. "You, huh? The guy who wanted to see the captain. Okay, you long-haired freak, you're gonna see the captain. The rest of you men, clean up this mess, every last bit of it, or I'll make you lick it up."

Fletch was thrust roughly out of the dining room, prodded down a corridor and into an elevator which took him to the floor where the deputy chief had his office. He waited in the small anteroom for a quarter of an hour, under guard, while the prosecution presented its case against him on the other side of the door marked Captain Arthur Deacon—Private.

When he was finally ushered in, he saw at a glance that he had already been convicted in absentia. Captain Deacon had the appearance of a hanging judge. He was a huge burly man with a completely bald head. As if to compensate for the loss, his beard, though closely shaven, was extremely dark and his eyebrows abnormally shaggy. The office suited its no-nonsense occupant, entirely functional, unimaginative in decor and nearly as spartan as the cells. There were floor-to-ceiling windows, however. Through them one could, smog permitting, glimpse the mountains. The most prominent of these, appropriately, was Mount Baldy.

Its human counterpart held a sheaf of papers which Fletch guessed was his dossier. Deacon raised his piercing gaze from them to their subject. "Chris Fletcher," he said, heavy lips curling as if the name tasted bad. "I hear you've been demanding preferential treatment. Well, Fletcher, I'm going to give it to you. Forty-eight hours in solitary. How does that suit you?"

"It doesn't. I'm hoping you'll turn me loose instead."

Deacon's lips writhed again, this time to form an ironic smile. "Sure you are. Funny I didn't think of that myself." He nodded at the guard.

"Let's go," the guard said, emphasizing the command with a poke in the ribs.

Fletch had not come this far and with such difficulty to be dismissed so quickly. "Please, Captain—at least let me explain a few things. That's the only reason I cranked it on in the mess hall, so I could rap with you."

He received a second, harder poke. Deacon forestalled a third by holding up his hand. "Man goes to that much trouble, he should get to speak his piece. But make it fast. I bore easy."

"Could I talk to you alone, sir? What I've got to say is very confidential."

"I'll bet." Nevertheless, Deacon made a dismissing gesture at the guard. Seeing him hesitate, he scowled. "Hell, Benny, I can handle this punk and ten like him. Wait outside."

"Thanks," Fletch said gratefully. "I promise you won't regret it."

"I promise you will—if you're wasting my time." Deacon leaned back in his swivel chair and folded his arms. "Shoot."

"It's absolutely imperative that I get out of jail immediately, Captain. I know—every man here feels the same way. The difference is that if you don't release me there's going to be a terrible crime committed. I'm the only one who can stop it."

"What sort of crime?"

"Kidnapping and probably murder."

"Yeah?" Deacon replied, plainly skeptical. "Who's the lucky victim?"

"I don't know."

"Then let's try an easier question. Who's going to commit this terrible crime? You do know that, don't you?"

"Yes. It was supposed to be me. You see, I joined this gang—I'm not really one of them even though they think I am—and they gave me the job of—"

"Aw, come on," Deacon interrupted, more in reproach than anger. "You trying to lay the groundwork for a psycho plea? Why bother?" He indicated the sheaf of papers on his desk. "I've gone through your jacket. You don't have too much to worry about. The only charge that'll stand up is clobbering Sergeant Quinsler. Considering you don't have any previous record, you'll likely get off with time served and probation. Just be a good boy and you'll be out of here inside a week at the latest."

"That'll be too late. You've got to believe me, Captain.

I'm trying to save somebody's life!"

He read the melodramatic line with all the acting skill he possessed. It didn't appear to be enough; Deacon continued to gaze at him with the same weary disbelief. Then the close-set eyes narrowed. "Convince me," he suggested softly.

It was all the invitation he needed. He began at the beginning, with Curt's murder, leading to his recruitment by General Sugarman and his successful penetration of the guerrilla tribe . . . concluding with the events of the previous evening when, on the verge of learning all, his premature arrest had ruined everything. He omitted only the part he had played in the bombing of COIN's headquarters, fearing that this—the one truly criminal act he had committed—might cause Deacon to see only the molehill and overlook the mountain.

Deacon listened intently but without interruption, obeying the first rule of police interrogation: Let the suspect talk. His expression betrayed neither acceptance nor incredulity. When Fletch had finished, he asked a single noncommittal question. "That all?"

"That's all. But surely you can see—"

"If that's all, then shut up. Give me a chance to think about it." He did so, brows furrowed. Finally he muttered, "That's a mighty slick story, Fletcher—or whatever the hell your name is—and you tell it well. But then, you say you're an actor so . . ."

"I'm not acting now, Captain. What do I have to do to convince you?"

"A little proof would help. Like, for instance, you claim to work for General Sugarman. Happens that I know damn near every man in his outfit and your name doesn't ring a bell."

"Well, I don't carry an ID card, for obvious reasons. But if you'll just pick up that telephone and call the general—"

"I could do that," Deacon conceded. "Except for one thing. General Sugarman isn't taking any calls."

"Why not?"

"He had a stroke about a week ago."

"My God!" Fletch breathed. Sugarman's cerebral accident had obviously occurred shortly after their telephone conversation—which solved the mystery as to why he had not alerted the police to the bombing. "That's just awful. Is he going to pull through?"

"No. He died yesterday. And since he's not around to back up your story—"

His initial reaction had been that Sugarman's incapacitation would make his job more difficult. Now he realized that Sugarman's death might well spell disaster. "Wait a minute," he said, trying to rally. "So the general can't vouch for me—there's got to be others at COIN who can. He must have told somebody about me, left some kind of record—"

"I'll say this for you, Fletcher. You don't give up easy."

He sensed that Deacon had made up his mind and, sensing it, grew desperate. "You can at least check, can't you? What sort of a cop are you, anyway? I've told you the truth! Okay, you don't have to take my word for a damn thing—but just stop sitting there on your fat ass, shaking your fat head, and start doing the job you're getting paid to do!"

Deacon came out of his chair with a snarl. "I promised to listen to you and I have. Now you listen to me. I don't need a punk to tell me what my job is and how to do it." He raised his voice to summon the guard. "Put him in the hole, Benny." He noted Fletch's quick glance around and interpreted it correctly. "Don't try it," he warned. "First, you'd never make it. Second, I am going to check you out—front, back and sideways. I've already got a damn good idea what I'll find but until I can prove it I'm putting you where I can't hear you squawk."

Relief made Fletch grin. "I love you, Captain. Even when you're angry."

"You think I'm angry now?" Deacon retorted. "You ain't seen nothing yet."

Fletch's new quarters were aptly named. Solitary detention was designed to impress troublemakers with the error of their ways. "The hole" was tiny, windowless and lacking all furnishings save the commode. Since the seat had been removed, he could not even use the porcelain receptacle as a chair. Neither could he use the floor as a bunk; the four-by-four cell prevented his stretching out in any direction. He could stand, squat or sit. During the next few hours, he did all three. However, he did not protest. He was confident of vindication. Such being the case, he could afford to take the long view.

He entered the hole around noon. He estimated that the hour was close to five when the guard finally released him from it. He was taken once again to the executive level. Deacon had shed his coat but not his hostile expression. However, the dossier on his desk had nearly doubled in size. Fletch waited serenely for the apology.

"Speaking of COIN," Deacon began abruptly, as if taking up their previous conversation at the spot where it had been interrupted, "suppose you tell me all about how you blew it up last week."

Fletch could not conceal a gulp of consternation. "I don't know what you mean," he replied weakly.

"Don't you? Well, while you're thinking up a better answer than that, let me bring you up to date. I've checked you out, just like I promised. First, I pulled the file on Curtis Orr. He wasn't murdered the way you claim. The verdict was accidental death. The possibility of homicide wasn't even raised."

"I explained to you that General Sugarman decided—"

"That's lie number one," Deacon went on, paying no attention to the interruption. "Lie number two—your claim to be a COIN agent. Nobody there ever heard of you."

"Didn't you ask them to check their records? I must be in there someplace!"

"There aren't any records to check—and you damn well know it. They all burned up in that fire you set. Which brings us to lie number three, the one you told just now. The people at COIN didn't recognize your name but they sure as hell recognized your picture." Deacon slammed his fist down on the dossier. "I've got sworn statements from at least a dozen people who have identified your mug shot as the guy who posed as a repairman the same day the bomb went off. How do you like them apples, sonny boy?"

"Give me a chance to explain," Fletch begged. "Sure, I planted the bomb. I did it to make myself look good to the guerrillas, the same reason I slugged Quinsler. But it was never supposed to go off. I phoned Sugarman to warn him so he could stop it in time. It's not my fault that his stroke loused things up."

Deacon sighed. "Sure, sure. You ready to make a statement?"

"You mean a confession? Hell, no! I haven't done anything, damn it!"

"You don't deserve it but I'll give you a piece of advice, take it or leave it. If you intend to stick with that frigging cock-and-bull story, get yourself a good lawyer. A damn good lawyer." He bellowed for the guard.

Fletch made one last try to sway the unimaginative officer. "Ask yourself this question, Captain. Why did I tell you any story at all, when it could only get me in trouble —unless it was the truth?"

"I'll tell you why. You're like a lot of these young punks, too clever for your own good. You thought you'd get a big laugh by giving us stupid cops the finger. Well, you had me going for a while but now it's my turn."

"Do anything you like with me. That doesn't matter. The only thing that matters is that you stop Gann. I've told you where he's holed up. Arrest him now, tonight, before it's too late!"

"Can't very well arrest people who don't exist, can I?" Deacon retorted. "I'm still way ahead of you, Fletcher. I sent a team dressed like construction workers to check out that so-called hideout. They didn't turn up a thing to show that anybody's been there inside a year except the rats. The place is as clean as a whistle." He nodded at the guard. "Bury him again, Benny."

"You can't leave it like that!" Fletch shouted as he was thrust toward the door. "I've got to get out of here, I tell you!"

Deacon smiled mirthlessly. "What's that they say in your racket? Don't call us, we'll call you."

Fletch was dragged back to solitary detention. This time he did not accept his confinement cheerfully. But though he yelled until his throat was hoarse and hammered on the door until his fists were sore, he discovered—as many men before him have discovered—that the poet had lied. Stone walls do a prison make . . . and iron bars a cage.

# Fourteen

DURING THE NEXT thirty-six hours, Fletch learned something else also. His gift for impudent invention, on which he had always relied, had its limits, after all. He couldn't con an empty cell or charm a locked door open. Not that he didn't try, anyway. His hunger strike was met with indifference, his terminal illness with scorn and his bribes with amusement.

"You'll be sorry!" he shouted at his jailers in a final burst of petulance. "I'll hold my breath till I turn blue!"

That childish threat, surprisingly, drew the strongest reaction. The guard who had the Sunday duty, a not unkindly officer nearing retirement age, told him to take it easy "because if you keep acting like this, they'll put you in restraint when you go to court—and that makes a lousy impression on the judge."

Fletch reluctantly accepted discretion as the better part of valor. Like it or not, he was stuck in jail until Monday morning. His sole hope now lay in convincing the judge if not of his innocence at least of his right to immediate bail. There might still be time to find the PTA—wherever they had gone—save Timmy and perhaps even the anonymous person called Mother. To this end, he transformed himself into a model prisoner for the balance of the weekend.

Monday morning finally came. Shortly after breakfast, he was taken from the hole to meet with the public defender, an underweight and overworked attorney named Swanson. Swanson was already acquainted with the charges against him and, with a score of other clients waiting, was interested only in dealing with them in the most expeditious manner. "Let me talk to the D.A.'s people," he suggested. "You know, explore the situation, see if we can't come to some sort of understanding where we plead you guilty to a lesser charge and get them to dismiss the rest. Otherwise, you'll be bound over for trial and, frankly, with the case they've got . . ."

Plea bargaining was a common (some said evil) practice, one of society's compromises whereby the ponderous machinery of justice was kept operable, if hardly the efficient instrument it was intended to be. Fletch didn't relish being a party to it, especially since he knew himself innocent. On the other hand, sacrificing his scruples was a small price to pay for his freedom. "Have it your way," he agreed unwillingly. "How soon can we get it over with?"

Swanson's reply horrified him. "Tuesday and Thursday are arraignment days. Court calendar's crowded as hell so you'd better figure on Thursday. That'll give me more time to wheel and deal, anyhow."

"Thursday! You're out of your mind! Don't you understand? All hell's about to break loose and if I'm not there to stop it people are going to die!" He pounded on the small table which separated them. He realized that he was behaving hysterically but in his desperation could not restrain himself. "Why won't anybody believe me, for God's sake?"

A guard stuck his head into the room, alarmed by the outburst. Swanson waved him back. "Shape up," he warned his client in a low voice. "I was told you had a screwy fixation about some kind of plot or the other. As your attorney, I strongly advise you to cool it and quick. If you persist in raving like a maniac, that's exactly how they'll treat you. Ever seen the psycho ward? Compared to it, the hole is the Beverly Hilton."

Fletch drew a deep breath. "Sorry. I'm not a maniac and I'm not raving. I'm not guilty of those charges, either, but that's beside the point. All that matters is that I get out of jail—not tomorrow, not Thursday, but today. Will you help me?"

"I'll do everything I can for you. But what you're asking is simply out of the question." Swanson put a comforting hand on his arm. "Your first time in stir, right? I can understand how you feel. Thursday looks like a thousand years away. It isn't. Believe me, you'll survive."

"Sure," Fletch said bitterly. "Me and who else?"

The conference over, he was returned not to solitary detention but to B-3 where his cell mates greeted him with respectful admiration. The rebellion in the mess hall had already become a minor legend with Fletch as its hero. They believed that he had scored a victory of sorts over their enemies. Fletch, however, knew that he had been thoroughly whipped. He repaid the adulation with a snarl, climbed into a bunk and sought the only solace still remaining, oblivion through sleep.

The afternoon newspaper informed him that Bruno Sledge had, as expected, been formally sentenced to the penitentiary for the rest of his natural life. Fletch read the headline with indifference; the game was over and he had lost. He was not allowed to forget it, though. His fellow prisoners made Sledge's fate the principal subject of conversation. Oddly enough, they held little sympathy for the condemned man. While they shared the same hatred for "the system," they considered his call to the barricades an unappetizing alternative. "Goddam commie" was their contemptuous verdict—which to Fletch summed up the futility of the urban guerrilla cause. If they could not inspire even the dregs of the society to rebel against it, what chance did they have with the rest? Unfortunately, wars frequently continue long after the possibility of winning them has vanished, with nothing to show for it except more casualties.

Lights in the cell block were extinguished at 10 P.M. Fletch had barely fallen asleep when they were turned on again. The loudspeaker ordered him forth. He stumbled into the freeway to the dire predictions of his cell mates that he was being returned to the hole, plus exhortations to "don't let the bastards hassle you, man!"

The officer in charge either did not know or would not reveal the reason for the summons. "Captain's orders," he said curtly. Fletch was led to the elevator. On the executive level most of the doors which lined the corridor were dark and Deacon's anteroom was empty. The private office beyond was neither. Despite the hour, Captain Deacon was still at work behind his scarred and littered desk. Not only that, he had company, a stocky man of about thirty-five, with the shoulders of a linebacker and the aggressively confident face of a surgeon. He swung around in his chair to study Fletch but did not rise or introduce himself.

Deacon dismissed the guard. As soon as the door closed, he said abruptly, "Okay, Fletcher. That story of yours— let's hear it again."

"What for? I've already told you everything there is to tell and nobody will believe it."

"Try me," the stranger suggested. He held up a wallet to which a badge was pinned. "Nicholas Vitullo, FBI. I'm agent-in-charge, L.A. office."

Fletch's surprise gave way to understanding. "FBI," he murmured. "It's happened, hasn't it?"

"What do you mean by 'it'?" Vitullo parried.

"Oh, let's not play cute. If the FBI's been called in, the magic word is kidnapping. Who did they grab?"

Vitullo and Deacon exchanged glances and Vitullo nodded. "The mayor," Deacon said. "The Honorable Otis Moran. He's been missing since about five o'clock this afternoon."

140

"Mayor Otis Moran—M.O.M." Fletch sighed. "Pappy told me I'd understand why they called him Mother."

"Mayor Moran left the civic center at four forty-five p.m., heading home to pack for his trip to Japan. He never got there. We found his Cadillac in Griffith Park a little after seven. There was a note in it stating the kidnappers' demands." Deacon fumbled among the papers on his desk. "You can read it for yourself."

"Never mind. I can tell you what it says. You release Bruno Sledge or they'll execute the mayor."

"Within twenty-four hours," Vitullo elaborated. "Sledge is to be flown out of the country, first stop Cuba via Mexico City. They were even thoughtful enough to provide us with the necessary airline timetables."

He recalled another timetable. "That's Pappy, all right."

Deacon growled, "Okay, spit it out. You warned me and I laughed at you. But if you heard as many fairy tales as I do, you'd have laughed too."

"What am I supposed to say, Captain?" He was unable to conceal his bitterness; the memory of the past three days was still too fresh. "Better luck next time?"

"Recriminations serve no useful purpose," Vitullo said impatiently. "Neither do mea culpas. We're faced with a fait accompli. The question of who may or may not be to blame for it really isn't important now."

"If it's important questions you want, try this. What are you going to do about it?"

"We're between a rock and a hard place. Otis Moran is no ordinary man. War hero, Congressional Medal winner, the best mayor this town's ever had and a cinch to be California's next governor—not to mention a personal friend of the President. You don't write off someone like that lightly. On the other hand . . ." He hesitated. "Since you're apparently one of Sugarman's people, after all, you're probably familiar with Policy X."

"Never heard of it."

"We've known that a political kidnapping was bound to happen sooner or later. We've also known that we had precious little chance of preventing it. The government simply doesn't have either the money or the manpower to throw a guard around every prospective victim. Instead, we have Policy X. X for Expendable. It was originally intended to cover only federal officials but in the last year it's been extended to top state and local officials as well. They've all been briefed on it, Moran included. Policy X can be summed up in one sentence: The government will do everything in its power to rescue the kidnap victim, including the payment of ransom, but it will not countenance any bargain which constitutes a threat to national security." Vitullo shrugged his broad shoulders. "The decision has been made. Releasing Bruno Sledge would constitute a threat to national security. Needless to say, that's confidential information."

"If you ask me, you're making a big mistake," Deacon said. "I say we should tell the kidnappers flat out that we won't trade, call their frigging bluff—"

"You're beautiful," Fletch said scornfully. "Can't you get it through your thick head that they're not bluffing?"

"Says who?" Deacon retorted. "It so happens that I've got a hell of a lot more experience in these things than the two of you put together and—"

"No one's questioning your experience, Captain," Vitullo soothed. "But these people aren't ordinary criminals. They're fanatics. Frankly, I believe they mean exactly what they say. Be that as it may, our job isn't to issue ultimatums. Our job is to track down the kidnappers and get Mayor Moran back before they kill him. To do that, we need your help, Fletcher."

Fletch laughed. "What's so damn funny?" Deacon demanded.

"Sorry, gentlemen, but I've got a warped sense of

humor. Two days ago I begged for the chance to help you before it was too late. For that I was roughed up, thrown in the hole, called everything from a liar to a psycho. Now, when it is too late, I'm suddenly not such a lousy freak, after all. I ought to tell you to go to hell."

Deacon reddened angrily; Vitullo retained his composure. "But you won't. First, because you're not that kind of man. And, second, because you've still got your own personal score to settle with the guerrillas."

There was a third reason also. "Okay, Mr. Vitullo, I'm in for the duration. But I demand my pound of flesh—about a hundred and five pounds, in fact. One of Gann's gang is a girl named Timmy Towne. Win, lose or draw, I want your word that she'll be let off the hook."

"Ansel Towne's daughter?" Vitullo's eyes widened. "What's she to you?"

"You wouldn't believe it if I told you. I hardly believe it myself. Is it a deal?"

"I'll go this far," Vitullo said slowly. "If Mayor Moran is released unharmed, the Towne girl will get immunity. Otherwise, she's as guilty of kidnapping and murder as the rest and she'll have to take the consequences. That's the best I can offer. Oh, and that all charges against you will be dropped in any case."

Fletch realized that haggling was pointless. The FBI agent did not have the authority to make a better bargain. "If you can't get five, take two. Time's short so let's head 'em up and move 'em out. I'll need my car."

"You can have anything you want—including a small army."

"No army. Not because I yearn to come on like the Lone Ranger but because this has got to be a solo. I'm banking that Pappy still considers me his fair-haired boy. If I show up with guns blazing and sirens blowing, he might just possibly revise that opinion and take out his chagrin on our beloved mayor."

"There's always the possibility that Moran is already dead."

"Not yet, he isn't. If and when Moran is killed, it'll be done in some spectacular and highly visible fashion. I know. I'm the one who's supposed to stage it."

"Any idea where they might be holed up?"

"Not the foggiest." Fletch studied the clock on the wall. "But I've got a shade under nineteen hours to find them. Do the papers have the story yet?"

"No. They've been told that the mayor has canceled his trip to Japan because of illness."

"Good. That should keep a lot of amateur detectives from getting in the way. One amateur is enough. Where's Bruno Sledge?"

This time it was Deacon who consulted the clock. "He's scheduled to leave for the north in about thirty minutes."

"Cancel it—and be sure the news media find out you have. It might make Gann think you intend to deal." Fletch considered. "That's about it. Except for one thing."

"Name it."

"This." He leaned across the desk and rubbed the startled Deacon's bald head vigorously. "Just for luck," he explained. "It really should be a polished stone—but I guess that's close enough."

# Fifteen

TEN MINUTES LATER he was breathing the heady air of freedom. His release was accomplished with as much stealth as if he had been escaping, Deacon dispatching the officers who might have seen and possibly wondered at his departure on various pretexts. Vitullo himself brought the Volkswagen to the exit of the basement garage where its owner lurked, and rode with him as far as the federal building.

"You're on your own now," he told Fletch in parting. "We'll keep our hands off until we hear from you."

Fletch didn't believe a word of it. The FBI agent was an experienced lawman, as tough as Captain Deacon and a good deal more subtle. He was not likely to risk all his eggs in such a flimsy basket. Fletch suspected that Vitullo, his promise notwithstanding, would attempt to keep him under surveillance. To test the theory, he drove about aimlessly for a while, watching his mirror for possible pursuit. Twice he thought he detected it but each time the other vehicle turned off in another direction after a few blocks. At last, reassured, he abandoned evasive action and set a course for his destination.

Given the size of the city and the number of its inhabitants, his chances of finding the guerrillas appeared almost nil, particularly since those he sought had ample reason not to wish to be found. Lionel Gann, like a good general, had moved his tiny army immediately after Fletch's arrest lest his erstwhile lieutenant should, wittingly or unwittingly, betray them. Where? It was a question for which he had no answer. The PTA and their hostage might be hiding anywhere—near at hand or fifty miles away, deep in a cave or high in a skyscraper, aboard a ship in the harbor or inside a house in the suburbs. The list of possibilities was virtually endless and it would take many times the eighteen hours at his disposal to explore even a fraction of them. It was foolish to suppose that Gann might have left a forwarding address for him . . . but he clung to the hope that Timmy had.

And so he returned to Angel Heights. Tonight the uncompleted urban renewal project more than ever resembled the former dwelling place of a vanished civilization. A late evening fog obscured the tops of the gutted buildings and eddied down the littered streets, enhancing the feeling of isolation. A few blocks away, beyond the fence, lived other human beings, eating and sleeping, watching TV and making love—but here, swathed in silence and the gray mist, it was easy for Fletch to imagine himself the last man on earth.

He climbed the fire escape to the second floor of the building which had been his home for the past ten days. Using his flashlight, he explored the room he and Timmy had shared. Only the faint outline in the dust created by their sleeping bags proved that it had been recently occupied. He scrutinized every inch of it, from the peeling wallpaper she had attempted to remove to the grimy windows she had planned to curtain, without finding the clue he sought. Still hopeful, he descended to the cellar.

The PTA's evacuation, if hasty, had been well executed. They had left nothing of their own behind. Gone were the boxes on which they had sat, the stove on which they cooked, the tub in which they washed their clothes and the rope on which they dried them. Even the doorless refrigerator which served as their arsenal had vanished. All that remained was the graffiti on the walls and the faint aroma of boiled cabbage in the air.

"Ten points for neatness," Fletch murmured.

He was not the only investigator on the scene. The rats, no longer deterred by a human presence, had invaded the cellar in search of food their enemies might have left behind. Lack of reprisals had made them bold. But not yet too bold; they scampered away when he stamped his feet, fleeing the probing beam of the flashlight as if its touch might prove fatal.

"Make that five points," he amended. The guerrillas had forgotten something, after all, the stub of a candle. The rats had found it first; the wax taper was gnawed nearly in two. Fletch lit it, anyway, since it offered more reliable illumination than his flashlight, whose batteries threatened to die at any moment. Holding the candle before him like an altar boy, he made a slow circle of the basement. A feeling of despair began to steal over him. There was no message.

He refused to accept defeat. Put yourself in Timmy's place, he argued. Would I run off without leaving some word for the one I love? Hell, no! Okay, then—where is it? He stared at the graffiti, those sometimes witty, often profane scribblings of which Timmy had been the most prolific contributor. He had read them before, looking for a recent addition and not finding it. On the possibility that he had missed one, he read them again. The result was the same . . . but, wait a minute—what was that?

In a corner, near the stairs, something new had been written and then erased. However, the eraser had removed not only the graphite but the underlying grime as well, leaving a faint blurred copy of the original. Lacking a pencil of his own, Fletch used the blackened end of a match to restore as many of the letters as his ingenuity could manage. He regarded the fragmentary result blankly. *n the      tain s nds a   dy . . .*

"On the mountain stands a lady!" he shouted suddenly. "Bless your cotton-pickin', rope-jumpin' heart!"

There could be no question as to the author. Timmy had left a message she felt sure he would understand—and Gann had ordered it removed, fearing that others might understand it also. The PTA's new hiding place was on a mountain! His elation faded a trifle as he realized that the city was virtually surrounded by mountains, from rounded foothills to lofty peaks. Without more specific directions, he was little better off than before. But since Timmy would have known that as well as he, Fletch commenced to search for a second clue.

It was so large he nearly missed it. Over the message Timmy had drawn a giant inverted V like a canopy, the mapmaker's symbol for a mountain. To the apex of the V was attached something—three somethings, in fact—which he could not decipher but which he felt sure was intended to distinguish this particular mountain from all others. Fletch puzzled over what the small figures represented. Television transmitters? Aircraft navigational beacons? Early warning radar stations? Water tanks? The answer continued to elude him. He ran his fingers lightly over the wall, in case touch might serve where sight did not. The pencil had gouged the plaster slightly.

"A cross," he murmured. Certainly, the Christian symbol was often found on mountaintops—and perhaps nowhere more frequently than in cult-ridden Southern California—a reminder, usually ignored, of the blood which had been shed for man's redemption. Their semi-isolation made them more popular with lovers than with worshipers, except at Easter. Fletch himself had visited (but never for religious reasons) several such locations, one within rifle shot of the frenzied Hollywood Freeway. Yet none boasted more than a single cross while Timmy's drawing indicated three.

He did not yet have the complete answer but at least he now had a piece of it. With persistence and a little luck, he might reasonably expect to find the rest. Convinced that he could learn no more here, he left the building to the rats and the area to the wreckers. He stopped in the first all-night service station he saw. The attendant furnished him with a map but no information. Like many Angelenos, he had been born elsewhere and knew little of his adopted city save for the neighborhoods in which he lived and worked and the freeway which connected them. A mountain with three crosses on it? Sorry, mister.

Fletch telephoned several churches. Four did not answer; from the fifth he got a recorded prayer and a request to call back in the morning. Most ministers, in common with other professional men, observed regular business hours. It occurred to him then that there was one type of minister who did not.

Like the all-night service station, the Good Shepherd Rescue Mission was open around the clock. Located in the heart of the city's skid row, it offered food, shelter and consolation to the derelicts sorely in need of all three. Nondenominational and supported by contributions, the mission did not charge for its services. The sign in the lobby read: *Salvation is free—He has already paid for it.*

The chaplain tonight was elderly and arthritic, yet chipper in manner as if to prove that neither condition distressed him. He admitted to being a clergyman—"twice retired"—and a native of the city. When Fletch informed him that he was looking for a mountain, the chaplain smiled. "Most men are, whether they realize it or not. 'I will lift up mine eyes unto the hills . . .' "

"My mountain has three crosses on it."

The chaplain's smile turned wistful. "So does mine." Yet his was not nearby but eight thousand miles away and was called Calvary. He knew of no local equivalent.

"There's got to be one," Fletch insisted with the dogged conviction of one who dares not believe otherwise. "Maybe the crosses aren't there any more. Maybe they just used to be, years ago, and the place still has the name—

149

Three Crosses Mountain, or something like that."

Again the chaplain started to shake his head. Then he hesitated. "You couldn't be thinking of Tres Cruces, surely?"

"Why the hell couldn't I? Sorry, padre, I'm a bit on edge. What's Tres Cruces?"

"Well, it isn't a mountain, more of a high mesa, actually. It was part of one of the old Spanish land grants, Rancho de las Tres Cruces. But it's never been used for religious observances or much of anything recently. There was a cattle ranch there years ago. And the movie studios used it for a western location at one time."

Fletch spread his map upon the desk. "Show me, please."

The chaplain drew a circle, no larger than a dime, around a blank spot on the map which lay close to the ocean, north of Malibu and west of Beverly Hills. Fletch blessed the providence which had led him to this particular place and this particular man. The area, undeveloped and uninhabited, was not identified by name on the map. Alone, he would have never found it. "What's up there? Any cabins, homes, that sort of thing?"

"I haven't been near there in ten years. The old ranch-house may still be standing. I wouldn't count on it, not after the last fire. It burned right through there, you know."

Fletch wrung the old man's hand. "You've been a lifesaver."

"You seem surprised," the chaplain replied dryly. "After all, isn't that what we're here for?"

When he left the rescue mission, Fletch noted a dark-colored sedan parked a half block away, the only other automobile on the street. He noted also that the sedan, which contained two men, pulled away from the curb as he did. It remained a discreet distance behind, never approaching close enough for him to read the license or to glimpse the occupants. He felt convinced now of what he had only suspected before: the FBI was following him. Yet at the moment he decided to confront his pursuers, the sedan surprisingly turned off down a side street. It did not reappear but shortly afterward a second car fell in behind him. When it too veered off, a third took its place. Fletch understood. To avoid detection, the government agents were operating in relays, passing the responsibility from one to the next like a baton. But since the surveillance was not continuous, how could they be confident that they wouldn't lose him during one of the intervals? Fletch thought he knew the answer to that too.

He drove into the huge self-service parking garage beneath Pershing Square and, temporarily free of the law's scrutiny, made a careful examination of the bus. He found the small metal box almost immediately, attached with adhesive pads to the undercarriage. It was, he guessed, a high frequency transmitter by which Vitullo's men could triangulate his position. His first impulse was to discard it but then a better idea occurred to him.

Another of the ubiquitous sedans was waiting to take up the chase when he left the garage. Fletch watched his rearview mirror until the headlights vanished. Before others could take their place, he sought out the nearest cab stand. "Can you deliver a package for me?"

The cabbie could and would, providing the fare was paid in advance. Fletch gave him his last five dollars, a distant and nonexistent address and watched the taxi roar off with the transmitter riding in its rear seat. When he felt sure that the ruse had succeeded, he left also, but in the opposite direction.

Yet he couldn't help wondering, during the long drive toward the ocean, if his cleverness might not be stupidity in disguise. He had deliberately cut himself off from reinforcements; whatever dangers lay ahead, he must face them alone. The reason could be summed up in one word: Timmy. Vitullo had promised to spare her under certain conditions. But Vitullo had already broken one promise. The FBI's prime objective was to save the kidnapped mayor, not his kidnappers. Should Fletch lead the federal agents to them, the pressure to attack would be well nigh irresistible. Otis Moran might survive a pitched battle—but would Timmy? Vitullo, no doubt, was willing to take that chance. Fletch was not. Alone and armed only with his own ingenuity, he had bested Lionel Gann before. He felt confident that he could do it again.

Obeying the chaplain's instructions, he approached his destination by way of Topanga Canyon, following the state highway north, then turning east on Tres Cruces Drive. The steep narrow road, winding up to the plateau two thousand feet above, was apparently little traveled and in need of repair. The mammoth brush fire which had swept these ridges and canyons three years earlier could still be traced by the dead and blackened trees and an occasional stone chimney, all that remained of some cabin or weekend retreat. The chaparral had grown up around these melancholy monuments, hiding most of the destruction while at the same time guaranteeing more destruction to come. Now it was green from the spring rains. Soon it would be dry, needing only a spark to touch it off, if not this year then the next or the one after. Small wonder that few of the survivors had chosen to rebuild homes which could be neither insured nor protected.

Fletch encountered no other vehicle on the rutted road or any evidence that one had recently passed this way. Nevertheless, he was convinced that he was nearing the PTA's new lair. Tres Cruces was the sort of hiding place he himself would have chosen, close to the city yet isolated from it, secluded by day and deserted by night. How had the guerrillas found it? Prior knowledge aside, the answer to that question might well lie with Rufus Wren and his proposed nine-and-a-half-volume history of the movies—since Tres Cruces had once been used for western location filming.

He halted at the lip of the mesa to reconnoiter. The fog lay beneath him. With the aid of the moonlight he could see a considerable distance in all directions. The road forked here. One branch dipped into another canyon, suggesting this to be an alternate route to the lowland. The other meandered off across the plateau, destination unknown. He followed the latter with headlights extinguished, grateful for the frequent passage of aircraft overhead which camouflaged the clatter of his smaller engine. He did not expect to take the enemy by surprise but neither did he wish to advertise his arrival too far in advance, lest they be panicked into some hasty and possibly fatal action.

Shortly he came upon the remnants of a fence, three slack strands of barbed wire stretching off on either side of the road. The gate it had supported was gone but another sort of barrier stood in its place, two large boulders which might have been put there recently. Since he could drive no further, he left the bus and set off on foot.

The road continued a gradual ascent to the crest of a brush-covered ridge. When he reached the summit, he saw that his search had been rewarded. Nestled in the shallow valley beyond was a ramshackle structure which once had been a ranchhouse but now could only be termed a ruin. The fire capriciously had spared it—but the buckling walls and sagging roof indicated that the end was not far off in any case. Behind it, a barn had already partially collapsed, canted drunkenly to one side as if nudged by a giant elbow. No light escaped from the boarded-over windows and the weeds growing tall around the crumbling porch appeared to be untrampled by human feet. What if I'm wrong, after all? he wondered.

A voice came out of the darkness, frightening in its unexpectedness but reassuring in its familiarity. "Fletch! Is that you?"

It was Timmy. She ran forward without waiting for his answer and flung her arms about him; he realized that she was armed with a sawed-off shotgun. "Oh, gosh!" she babbled happily, midway between laughter and tears. "It's really you! You're here! I was afraid you'd never find me. When did you get out of jail? How are you? How did you ever know where I was?"

He didn't bother to explain since the tumbling questions were an expression of relief, not curiosity. "I promised I'd come back for you, didn't I? Where's everybody?"

"Inside. Except Injun—he's patrolling back of the house."

Only Timmy was aware of his presence so far. Fletch was sorely tempted to whisk her away in the waiting automobile. But he could not; her life was forfeit if Moran died, and that was one promise he felt sure Vitullo would keep. He opened his mouth to ask if the mayor was still alive, then shut it just in time. Since the kidnapping was a tightly guarded secret, he dared not reveal any knowledge of it. To do so was to invite someone to inquire how he knew—and to come to the inevitable conclusion that it was the police who had told him. Instead, he asked, "What are you doing out here in the boondocks, anyway? That's the crummiest-looking motel I ever saw."

"Oh, you missed all the action," Timmy told him. "You know that heavy job we were getting ready for? You'll never believe what it turned out to be."

"Try me."

"Well, it was to take a hostage to exchange for Bruno. Fletch, it's the mayor himself, Otis Moran! How about that?"

Her prideful exhilaration surprised him. Timmy might have been boasting about a childish prank rather than the commission of a capital crime. It was safe now to ask his previous question. "Is he still alive?"

"Huh? What do you mean? We're not going to snuff

him, for God's sake! Pappy explained it to us very, very carefully. We're just going to keep him under wraps until the Toppies turn Bruno loose."

"And if they don't turn Bruno loose?"

"Why, they will," Timmy replied positively. "Why shouldn't they? I mean, they're not about to let a man like Mayor Moran get jobbed. He's too big and important."

Her naïveté made him sigh. Gann had succeeded in convincing Timmy—and perhaps others of the PTA as well—that it was all a game, only a shade more sinister than Run Sheep Run. Undoubtedly, he feared that the less committed might balk otherwise. Once the deed was done, guilt would guarantee their loyalty. "Listen to me, Timmy," he began, seeking the words which would awaken her not only to Moran's peril but her own.

On the path ahead, a shadow moved. From the darkness, a male voice whispered, "Hold it right there or you've bought it." Injun, hearing Timmy's welcoming screech, had come to investigate.

"Cool it," Timmy replied. "Don't you recognize him? It's Fletch!"

Injun advanced cautiously. In addition to the ubiquitous knife, he also carried a pistol. He lowered the weapons with reluctance and Fletch thought it fortunate that Timmy and not he had been the sentry. "The big thumper himself," Injun murmured, no welcome in his voice. "Figured we'd lost you, Fletch. How'd you find us?"

"It wasn't so hard. I just followed my nose."

"Funny as ever, ain't you? Well, what're you standing out here for? Better report to Pappy. He's gonna be mighty surprised to see you."

Fletch held on to Timmy's hand; now that he had found her, he did not intend to be separated from her again. "Announce me, sweetheart. Injun won't mind taking over your post for a few minutes."

"Swive you," Injun growled. However, he stepped aside

to allow them to pass. "Make it snappy, huh? I'm already pulling an extra trick so Rufus can watch his goddam movie."

He trailed them toward the ranchhouse, making private conversation impossible. Fletch did what he could. Out of the corner of his mouth, he said softly, "Still remember what I said about you sticking to me, no matter what?"

"Huh?" Timmy asked sharply and he couldn't be sure she had understood him. There was no opportunity to repeat. They were already mounting the rickety porch. Timmy knocked on the door. On the other side of the panel Lionel Gann replied with a cautious "Yeah?"

"Open up, Pappy. We've got a visitor. Fletch's come back!"

Gann's voice rose incredulously. "Fletch!" The door opened a crack on screeching hinges to frame the ascetic bearded face. "Well, I'll be damned. The prodigal returneth. Come in, come in!"

The room was lit by a single candle, the air hot and filled with the sweetish aroma of marijuana. It was the former parlor of the ranchhouse and once perhaps had been comfortable, even attractive, in a rough-hewn fashion. But that was long ago. Now the beams were festooned with cobwebs and the dust of many years lay everywhere. Vandals had scrawled their names and their vulgarities over the huge stone fireplace with spray paint in pitiful attempts at immortality. Others had pried up a number of the floor boards for less discernible reasons, making footing perilous. The parlor's present occupants had done nothing to tidy up the room. Their only contribution had been to nail blankets over the windows to prevent light from escaping. Since this also prevented fresh air from entering, it could hardly be considered an improvement.

The television perched on the wide hearth, its back to him. Beside it an open box which had once contained toilet tissue held the PTA's supply of dynamite, blasting caps and ammunition, depleted by the attack on COIN but still formidable. Beyond it, in the glow cast by the screen, sat Choogle, Blossom, Midge and Rufus Wren. They stared at the newcomer, eyes wide and lips parted, as if seeing a ghost. Fletch's quick inventory did not discover Otis Moran—but the door to the room beyond was closed and bolted, hinting that the mayor of Los Angeles lay captive behind it.

He gave the guerrillas a cheery salute. "Remember me?"

Gann chuckled. "You'll never believe this, but we were just talking about you. Right, gang? It's absolutely eerie, you popping in at this very moment."

"Hope I didn't spook you."

"Are you kidding?" Gann put a comradely arm around his shoulders. "We're watching the windup of the Late Show. A blue ribbon occasion—it's one of the few flicks Rufus hasn't seen before. Midge, dust off a seat for the guest of honor."

The others slid aside to make a place for him. Fletch sat down, wondering at their lack of curiosity about his return. "Good show?" he asked Wren.

"Scuzzy but fascinating," Rufus replied in an odd voice.

Fletch glanced at the screen. His heart gave a sudden sickening thud and then commenced to race frantically. Tonight's late movie was *Kiss Me or Kill me*. The face which gazed back at him belonged to a young actor named Chris Fletcher.

# Sixteen

FLIGHT WAS OUT of the question. He was surrounded on all sides; his enemies were armed and he was not. He felt sure that the guerrillas had already recognized his image upon the screen. They watched him covertly for the guilty start which would confirm the identification. Nothing remained except to bluff it through, on the faint chance that he might thereby raise a doubt in their minds. He stared at the picture with an expression of mild boredom, emphasized with an occasional yawn. As the minutes dragged by without the expected accusation, he began to hope that the bluff might work.

Timmy, of all people, was the one who called it. "It just came to me!" she exclaimed. "That guy seems so darn familiar and I couldn't figure out why. Now I know—he looks like you, Fletch."

"That budgy kid?" he retorted with pretended indignation. "Give me a break, will you?"

But the damage was done. "I commented on the resemblance earlier," Gann said. "As a matter of fact, we all did. Same face, same voice—why, he's a dead ringer for you."

"Maybe I should sue," Fletch replied weakly.

"Well, you've got quite a case—because he's using your name, too. Rufus was the one who pointed it out to us on the credits. We thought it was real funny. At first."

"Now wait a minute, Pappy—"

"You wait. The picture's nearly over and I want to see how it ends."

Gann was toying with him, forcing him to sit there and sweat while—a final twist of the knife—watching his fictional counterpart vanquish his enemies singlehanded and emerge with a smile on his lips, a girl in his arms and the world in his pocket. The movie, like most, postulated a fantasyland where villainy was punished and heroism rewarded. Fletch had not believed in it at the time. He believed in it even less now as he waited for the resolution of his own melodrama.

The music swelled to its conclusion, then ended in midbar as the station cut abruptly to a commercial announcement. Gann turned off the set. "I do like movies with a message—and that certainly had one, wouldn't you say? Rufus, you'd better relieve Injun before he blows his stack."

A silence followed Wren's departure. Fletch broke it by clearing his throat. "I'll bet you're dying to hear how I spent my weekend."

"We can hold out if you can." Gann was postponing the showdown until Injun was there to share it. When the bare-chested hatchet man finally joined them, he smiled at Fletch. "The stage is yours. Maybe I should say the screen. Suppose you begin by telling us how you happened to be in that picture. Or are you still claiming that actor was the winner of the Chris Fletcher look-alike contest?"

"Oh, it was me, all right," Fletch replied with a carefully calculated blend of candor and embarrassment. "Anybody care for my autograph?"

"We'll settle for your explanation."

"Well, I was hoping to keep that particular skeleton locked in my closet but since you've already seen it . . . It happened about five years ago. I was the golden boy of the Berkeley drama department and this producer came up there scouting for an unknown to appear in his picture. He

159

signed me. I had eyes to be the big star, you know? But after I'd made the Hollywood scene it was all so damn plastic that I told them to shove it. I hustled back to Cal and forgot the whole ugly mess. Not that anyone tried to stop me. I guess that picture proves what a lousy actor I am."

"Don't be modest," Gann reproved. "I think you're one hell of an actor. You've been acting up a storm ever since you joined us. You're acting right now. If you could put it on film, you'd win an Oscar sure." He plucked the sawed-off shotgun from Timmy's grasp and thrust the muzzle against Fletch's stomach. "Show's over, Fletch."

The others were frozen statues. Only Timmy, bewildered by events she did not understand, protested. "Pappy—what are you doing? Don't you believe him?"

"I'll tell you what I believe," Gann said, without moving his eyes from Fletch's face or the muzzle from his stomach. "I believe he's working for COIN. Sugarman planted him in the PTA to spy on us. He knew we might not buy any of his regular goons so he went outside the organization and hired an actor for the job."

"Aren't you forgetting something?" Fletch objected. "Think back. Who was it blew up COIN's headquarters?"

"That's right!" Timmy chimed in eagerly. "That should prove that he's really one of us."

Gann paid no attention. "I want the truth," he warned. "One more lie and I'm going to blow you apart."

His voice held a terrible ring of sincerity. Fletch let his shoulders sag in pretended surrender. The truth Gann demanded would seal his doom as certainly as another evasion—but perhaps a half truth might win him a reprieve. "Hell, I'm not about to argue with a shotgun. I have been gaming you. I'm not what I made out to be. But I'm not what you think, either."

The pressure against his belly eased slightly. "Keep talking."

"I am an actor—and a mighty broke one. I never went to Berkeley. But the law didn't send me after you. I'm working for Ansel Towne. He hired me to find his little girl and try to wean her away from her evil companions." He heard Timmy's incredulous gasp but dared not look at her lest his expression betray him. "I didn't plan on getting mixed up in your scruffy war, Pappy. I could care less about it—or you, for that matter."

"You're still lying," Gann said, but with less conviction than before. "Do you actually expect us to believe you'd put your life on the line for the sake of a few bucks?"

"Who said it was a few bucks? Anyway, I didn't look at it like that. I saw it as just another acting job. And a damn sight better paid than most."

"Well, I guess it really doesn't matter much," Gann decided. "A spy's a spy, no matter who hires him. You are mixed up in our war, Fletch, whether you planned it or not. It's too late to declare yourself a neutral."

"Blast him," Injun urged eagerly.

"What do you gain by killing me?" Fletch argued.

"Maybe nothing. But I don't see we stand to lose anything, either."

"I'll show you a way to make a profit. Let me go and take Timmy with me and you can have the fifty grand Ansel Towne is paying me."

"No!" The emphatic refusal came not from Gann but from Timmy; the word seemed to explode from her lips. "I won't go anywhere with you! I'd die first! You used me, you lied to me, you even made love to me—all for money! How could you be so, so . . ." Anger choked her.

"That isn't true, Timmy." He could not allow her to believe that, whatever the cost. "Sure, I set out to con you. But the joke's on me. I fell for my own con. That's why I came back for you. I love you."

His answer was a stinging slap across the mouth delivered with all the strength she could muster. "Liar!" she blazed. "Liar, liar, liar!" She raised her hand for another blow, then suddenly turned away and commenced to cry. "Oh, God!" she moaned. Her body shook with great racking sobs.

One or two of the others stirred uneasily, moved by her distress. Blossom slid closer in an attempt to comfort her. Gann, unmoved and unmoving, said, "Regarding your proposition, I think Timmy has answered for all of us."

"Blast him," Injun said again.

"Any objections?" There were none. Timmy, close to hysteria, didn't appear to understand the question. Of those who did, only Blossom failed to nod. She gave Fletch a glance of mute apology and stared at the floor, sympathetic but too weak to stand alone against her comrades.

"Seems to be unanimous," Gann declared. "Except for Rufus—and his vote wouldn't change the result, anyway."

"What're you waiting for?" Injun asked in a voice made guttural by anticipation. "Do it now and get it over with."

"Don't rush me. Fletch still has a few things to tell us. Like what he did to get the pigs to turn him loose. And how he managed to find us when we didn't leave any trail to follow."

"The pigs didn't turn me loose," Fletch told him. "I pleaded guilty to slugging Quinsler and, seeing as how I didn't have any previous record, the judge suspended my sentence."

The judge also give you directions on how to get here?"

"I got my directions off the cellar wall. Sure, I know you tried to erase them but you didn't do a very good job of it. Once I figured out the three crosses part, the rest was easy."

Gann regarded him with grudging respect. "Damned if you don't make me wish we were on the same side."

"Maybe it's not too late. I'd a hell of a lot rather be a live guerrilla than a dead neutral."

"No way. Even if you mean it—which I doubt—I'd

never be able to turn my back on you." Yet he surprised Fletch by removing the shotgun from his stomach. "I'm going to be just like the judge—suspend your sentence. We can use a second hostage. In case the mayor's friends decide to drag their heels, your body might convince them that we mean business. But if you're lucky, that won't be necessary."

Since he knew that the terrorists' demands had already been rejected, Fletch could find little cause for optimism. Yet even a few hours were preferable to none at all. He managed a wan smile. "Well, if that's your best offer . . ."

"Aw, hell!" Injun exclaimed, disgusted at being deprived of his satisfaction. "You gone soft, Pappy? I say scrub the nurd now before he makes us more trouble."

"Murder should serve a useful purpose," Gann told him as if lecturing a backward pupil. "It should be an act of strength, not a confession of weakness. Kill a man because you're afraid of him and you admit you're a coward. Kill him for revenge and you admit you're stupid because a clever man would make him suffer, instead. Murder is an art, or at least it should be. An artist uses it judiciously, at the right time and for the right reason . . . But I guess you'll never understand that, will you?" He turned abruptly to Blossom. "The party's getting dull. Play us something."

The incongruous request took her by surprise. "Huh? You mean, right now?" Gann nodded and Blossom, eager to cater to her lord's whim, unslung the guitar she carried on her back. "What'd you like to hear, Pappy?"

"Make it your choice." However, she had strummed only a few preliminary chords before he shook his head. "Something's wrong with your guitar. Let me have it." He examined the instrument for a moment, then deliberately smashed it against the floor, severing the neck from the body. Holding the two parts, connected now only by the six useless steel strings, he said, "Yeah, something's wrong with it, all right."

Blossom gaped at him with the shocked incredulity of a child who has seen her most precious toy wantonly destroyed. "Pappy," she whispered. "What'd you want to do that for?"

"I didn't like the way it played. It'd gone sour. Like you, Blossom."

"I—I don't know what you mean."

"Think hard. Do you suppose I've forgotten who it was that vouched for Fletch that first night? Tell me again how well you knew him up at Berkeley."

"I guess I made a mistake," Blossom mumbled, unable to meet his accusing eyes. "I thought I remembered him but—"

"You lied. You'd never seen him before and you knew it. And because you lied, he was able to worm his way into the PTA. Otherwise, I'd have booted him out on his ass. Admit it, Blossom. You lied to me."

Blossom twisted from side to side, a terrified animal seeking escape from the trap. Finding none, she commenced to whimper. "So maybe I did fake it. I didn't mean any harm by it, Pappy, honest to God I didn't! I was just trying to look important so you'd love me like I love you. Anyway, it was Timmy who—"

"Timmy made a bad mistake. But she didn't know any better. You did know better. You deliberately jeopardized the security of our mission and the lives of your friends. That makes you a traitor. As far as I'm concerned, there's nothing worse."

"I didn't know what I was doing! I didn't think!" She crawled toward Gann, her hands reaching for his as if physical contact might re-establish the bond between them. "I'm so sorry, Pappy! Please, please forgive me!"

Gann sighed. "I'm fond of you, Blossom. I still am, even now. But treachery's the one thing that can't be forgiven." In a sudden swift movement, he snared her throat with the guitar strings and twisted them tight. Blossom's face contorted as the steel wires bit into her flesh. Her slight body arched, fighting to break free, while her fingers clawed ineffectually at the six-strand noose.

Fletch sat paralyzed, believing that Gann meant merely to frighten the girl. Then he saw the coldly glittering eyes and he knew better. He lunged at the executioner in a desperate attempt to save the victim. A gun butt struck the nape of his neck, a blow which sent him sprawling. He thought he heard Timmy scream. Dazed but not unconscious, he struggled to rise. A second blow ended all thought of either rescue or resistance.

Awareness returned slowly. With it came pain. His head throbbed so badly that he had difficulty focusing his eyes. As that ache commenced to subside somewhat, he discovered others elsewhere, in his back and legs and shoulders. When he tried to shift his position, he made another discovery. He was spread-eagled on some sort of hard narrow platform, his ankles and wrists lashed securely to its corners. He had the sudden chilling thought that it was a crude altar and he the human sacrifice upon it.

He raised his head quickly. Although the movement made him groan, he was relieved to learn that the imagined altar was, in fact, a wooden bunk, sans springs or mattress. He lay upon its bare slats, which were made more uncomfortable by being spaced several inches apart like a picket fence. Above him hung a kerosene lantern. By its light he could determine that he was no longer in the parlor of the old ranchhouse. His captors had carried him into the locked room beyond.

He was not the room's only prisoner. Nearby stood a second bunk. Upon it lay a second man, older and smaller but similarly trussed. His eyes were covered with a grimy blindfold. He turned his sightless face in the direction of the groan. "Hey," he called in a whisper. "Can you hear me? Who are you? Say something, damn it!"

Fletch's lips were puffy; when he licked them, he tasted

blood. "I can hear you, Mayor. My name's Fletcher. You don't know me but, believe it or not, I came here to rescue you."

There was a silence and then Otis Moran chuckled. "Well, what are you waiting for?"

"I've run into a slight problem. Now I need rescuing myself."

"How about the police?" Moran asked hopefully. "Since you're here, they must have this place sealed off."

"Afraid not. They're not even close. I was foolish enough to believe I could handle the job alone."

"Do they intend to pay the ransom?"

Fletch sighed. "I seem to have nothing but bad news for you, Mayor."

He could imagine Moran's despair; however, the mayor conquered it swiftly. "Policy X," he murmured. "Well, so be it. Do you think these animals will actually go so far as to kill me?"

"Yes," Fletch said simply. There was no point in sugar-coating the facts, either for Moran or for himself.

"The hell they will," Moran replied defiantly. "I've been through two wars, Fletcher. A lot of real men have tried to scrag me and couldn't."

"This is a different kind of war, Mayor."

"War is war, no matter where it's fought or who fights it. Those spoiled brats—calling themselves a guerrilla army! They haven't learned the first thing it takes to be a guerrilla, and that's to Know Your Enemy. They don't know us at all. They think that all they have to do is to set off a few bombs and we'll hand over the world to them. Fat chance! Nobody handed it to us. We got it by starting at the bottom, putting in our time and paying our dues. Anybody who figures to take it away from us is going to have to do the same."

"You won't get an argument from me. But at the moment I'm not as much interested in who's going to win the war as who's going to survive it."

Below the blindfold, Moran's lips curved into a grin. "Me too, Fletcher. You got any bright ideas on that subject?"

"Our bunks are about a yard apart and roughly parallel. If we both work at it, maybe we can hitch them close enough so you can untie me, or vice versa."

"Like this?" Moran strained upward against his bonds while simultaneously throwing his body in Fletch's direction. The bunk moved a fraction of an inch closer.

"Like that." He began to do the same. They worked in a silence broken only by their labored breathing. The ropes bit into their wrists and ankles and the slats punished their backs but neither man voiced a complaint, preferring to conserve both breath and energy. Their progress was agonizingly slow. The bunks were heavy and the floor uneven. At the end of ten minutes, they succeeded in reducing the distance between them by less than a foot.

"How we doing?" Moran panted.

"We're getting there," Fletch told him with a confidence he didn't feel. He estimated that it would take another half hour at least before they were within touching range. And that was only the first small step on the road to freedom. Even if he should reach the knot which bound the mayor, he was not sure he could untie it; his hands felt numb and weak. Sweat poured down his forehead and into his eyes. He closed them to ease the sting and continued the struggle.

"Taking a trip?" a voice asked. Fletch raised his head and saw Injun grinning down at him. He was not sure how long Injun had been standing there. Engrossed in his labor, he had not heard the door open. Moran, though unable to see the unwelcome intruder, recognized disaster also. He greeted it with a muttered oath.

"Lemme help," Injun suggested mockingly. He moved the bunks even farther apart than they originally had been, more than canceling out the accomplishments of the past fifteen minutes. "Good thing I aced in. You might have taken a flaming spill." Fletch saw then what the side of the bunk had prevented his seeing before. Between him and Moran lay a gaping jagged hole where the flooring had collapsed. The gulf was too wide to bridge even without Injun's interruption. The enterprise had been doomed from the beginning.

"Yeah," Injun continued. "I had a hunch you'd be cranking something on. I ducked out on the burial detail to take a look."

"Then he actually killed her," Fletch murmured. Thinking only of his own life, he had nearly forgotten Blossom's. "That poor kid."

"She wasn't good for much anyhow." Injun accompanied the callous epitaph with a shrug. "Now it's your turn, Fletch. I still ache like hell where you kicked me. Wasn't sure I'd ever get the chance to pay you back. But, like they say, the sun don't always shine on the same dog." He withdrew his knife from his belt.

"You kill me and there'll be hell to pay," Fletch warned. "Pappy's orders were to keep me alive, remember?"

"Well now, I've had just about a bellyful of Pappy's orders. He ain't God, the way he tries to pretend. I figure to start running things around here directly."

Fletch had labored cunningly and long to turn the servant against his master. Now he realized that he had succeeded too well. "If you're going to buck Pappy, you'll need all the help you can get. I'll throw in with you and together—"

"Shove it, buddy. I don't need you. Anyhow, I think you got the wrong idea. I don't aim to cash you in. Like Pappy said, if you really want revenge, you don't total your man. You make him suffer." Pretending to study the glittering blade, Injun mused, "Pretty little tool, ain't it? No end to the things you can do with it. Used to have one

168

like it back home on the farm for gelding the stock. You ever seen that done, Fletch? I got to be real good at it, good and fast. Been a long time but I'll bet it'll come back to me."

"My God!" Moran cried in a voice which shook with horror. "You can't do a thing like that!" Fletch's throat was too paralyzed to say anything at all.

"Ain't no big thing, Mayor. Some of the feisty ones— the big boss hogs especially—they'd fight it and scream bloody murder. But afterward, hell, Mr. Hog was just as sweet as a little ol' puppy dog. Took the meanness clean out of him. They say a man ain't much different from a hog in a lot of respects." Injun paused thoughtfully. "Except maybe a man remembers the way he used to be where a hog don't."

Fletch had been prepared to die, if not willingly at least with fortitude. Facing the loss of his manhood, he was seized by an atavistic horror as old as the race itself, stripping him of both courage and dignity. As Injun bent over him, he screamed.

"Ain't even touched you yet," Injun reproved with a grin. He used the knife to sever his victim's belt. The point pricked flesh as he commenced to slit the denim jeans. "Sharp, huh? Better be glad it is. A dull blade's really brutal."

"What's happening?" Timmy stood in the open doorway, staring at the two men. "I heard a scream."

"What you heard ain't nothing to what you're gonna hear. I'm about to square accounts with ol' Fletch. If you wanna watch, stick around. If you don't, bug off."

She came forward slowly. Her face was pale and tear-streaked but she had recovered from her earlier hysteria. "What are you going to do to him?" Injun told her; Timmy's expression did not change. "I see."

"For God's sake, Timmy, help me!" Fletch begged in a voice he did not recognize as his own. "Don't let him butcher me!"

Her reply blasted his last faint hope. "Help you? Sure —I'll help you the way you helped me." She looked at Injun. "Is it very painful?"

"It'll do till the real thing comes along. Get a load of his face when the knife goes in."

Timmy caught his arm. "I've got a better idea."

"You wanna do the job yourself? No dice. He's mine."

"He's mine too. I want you to make love to me. Right here where he can watch. That's why I hurried back ahead of the others."

"Hey," Injun said softly. "Finally coming around, huh? Sure thing, babe, just as soon as I finish with the chores."

"Now," Timmy told him firmly, "or not at all. I want my kicks too. I want him to see what he's going to be missing for the rest of his life."

Injun started to shake his head, then hesitated, intrigued by the cruel proposal. "Heavy," he admitted. "Kinda puts the frosting on the cake, so to speak." He flipped the knife into the air; it came to rest upright in the slat between Fletch's legs. "Guess we'd better shut the door, being as how this is a private performance."

As he turned away, unbuckling his snakeskin belt, Timmy grabbed for the knife. Her action was a fraction of a second premature. Injun saw her lunge from the corner of his eye. He spun around, quick as a cat. Their hands closed upon the weapon almost simultaneously. For an instant, the man and the woman struggled for possession above the bunk on which Fletch lay, helpless to intervene. The man's strength was far greater; he wrenched the knife from Timmy's fingers. The victory cost him his balance. Stumbling backward, he blundered into the jagged hole between the two bunks, and fell headlong. He sprang to his feet immediately, apparently unhurt. Then Fletch saw the knife. Injun still gripped it tightly but now the blade was no longer visible. Falling, he had impaled himself upon it; the hilt protruded from his bare chest. He looked down at it stupidly as if puzzled by its presence there. With something akin to indignation, he yanked the knife from its scabbard of flesh. A gush of blood followed it, like wine from a bottle when the cork is removed; though he pressed his hands against it, the crimson tide continued to flow. Injun sat down abruptly, only the top of his head visible above the splintered floor boards. Then that too disappeared.

Timmy huddled against the wall where the struggle had flung her, too dazed to realize that she had won it. "The knife!" Fletch said sharply. "Get the knife, Timmy, and cut me loose!"

She stared at him with the uncomprehending expression of one just awakened from a deep sleep. He had to repeat the order more emphatically before she understood it. Her fingers were shaking so violently that she could barely control them. When at last she managed to free one of his hands, drawing blood in the process, Fletch took the knife from her and completed the job.

He massaged his arms to relieve their numbness. As sensation began to return, he used them to hug his savior. "Bless you," he murmured. "Bless you."

"I couldn't let him hurt you," she explained in a quavering voice—as if any explanation were necessary. "I don't care if it was all a lie. I still love you. I can't help it!"

"It wasn't all a lie, Timmy." There was no time to say more. Moran, writhing in an agony of apprehension, was demanding loudly to know what had happened. "Shut up," Fletch told him as he hacked away the ropes which bound the other man. "No offense, Mayor, but we're not out of the woods yet. Timmy—close that door."

Moran tore off the blindfold and stared at the allies he was seeing for the first time. "Where are the rest of them?"

"One's down in the hole. The other four are out digging

a grave."

Moran was tough. The terror of the past few hours, combined with the realization that there was more terror yet to come, might have shattered an ordinary man. But ordinary men do not win the Medal of Honor or claw their way to the top of the political heap. He managed a grim chuckle. "Theirs or ours?"

Fletch motioned him to be still and clamped one hand over Timmy's mouth to muffle the sobs she could not control. In the silence, they could hear the clatter of feet upon the rickety porch, followed by the squeal of rusty hinges as the ranchhouse door was opened. Moran's question would shortly be answered. Lionel Gann and his depleted but still dangerous army had returned.

# Seventeen

GANN'S VOICE CAME PLAINLY from the next room. "Where the hell is everybody? Injun, you in there?"

The door between them could not be barred from the inside. Since silence would invite investigation, Fletch replied in what he hoped was a fair imitation of Injun's twang. "Yo, Pappy. I'm busy."

"What's up?" Gann demanded irritably. "Hey, you seen Timmy?"

Fletch removed his hand from her mouth. "Say something," he whispered.

Timmy's voice trembled but did not break. "I'm busy too, Pappy. No fair peeking."

They heard Wren's high-pitched giggle. Gann, not amused, growled, "Knock it off, you two. We got more important things to do."

"Give a guy a break," Fletch grumbled. He watched Moran, who was attempting to remove the boards which covered the window. They resisted his efforts; it would take a pry bar to free them. The mayor spread his hands in a gesture of defeat. His lips formed the words "What now?"

The only avenue of escape led through the door—and beyond it lay the enemy. The two forces were nearly equal in numbers but not in firepower. Gann and his followers were heavily armed; their only weapon was the knife. "Timmy, you go out there. Tell Pappy that Injun'll be along in a minute. Then say you need to go to the bathroom and duck out. The keys are in the bus. Drive like hell to the nearest phone and call the cops."

Timmy shook her head. "Pappy moved the bus around back so nobody would spot it. He's got the keys. But maybe—if I could grab a gun . . ."

"You ever used one?" Moran inquired. When she hesitated, he grimaced. "Forget it, young lady. You'll only get yourself hurt." He tapped Fletch's shoulder. "I say you and I should rush them and hope for the best."

"You've got guts, Mayor. But they've got shotguns."

"You suggesting we give up? Not me!"

"I suggest we play Pappy's own game. It's called Take a Hostage. Put your blindfold on and lie down again. Timmy, when I give the signal, you open the door and tell Pappy the mayor is demanding to speak with him. If we can get him to step in here by himself—"

"Did you hear me?" Gann called loudly from the parlor, his patience exhausted. "I mean now, not a week from Tuesday, damn it!"

Fletch flattened himself against the wall next to the door jamb. He glanced at Moran, who was hastily arranging himself on the bunk in an approximation of his former position, then nodded to Timmy. She opened the door halfway. "Can you come here a sec, Pappy? The mayor says he wants to tell you something."

"Like what?"

Timmy's eyes flicked instinctively to Fletch for guidance. He prayed that Gann would not notice. I don't know, he mouthed. "I don't know," Timmy repeated obediently. On her own, she added, "He won't tell anybody but you. He says it's important."

Gann seemed reluctant. Then Fletch heard the floor boards creak, coming closer. He motioned Timmy to step back and waited, every muscle tensed, poised to spring at the first sight of his prey.

174

The prey was wary. Gann stopped short of entering the room, peering through the narrow aperture as if scenting a danger he could not see. The sight of Moran still spread-eagled on the bunk reassured him. He opened the door wider and took a step forward. "Okay, Mayor, what—"

At the same instant, his eyes fell upon the second bunk and found it empty. He flung himself backward, slamming shut the door. Fletch, grabbing for his throat, collided with the panel instead. He seized the knob, thinking to pursue. Then reason reasserted itself. He dodged to one side. His caution was justified. There was an angry blast of sound and a dozen or more small jagged holes appeared magically in the wood, chest-high.

Moran grunted and Fletch feared that he had been hit by the shotgun pellets. "Splinters," the mayor explained tersely. At the sound of the scuffle, he had leaped up in order to join it. There was a gash on his cheek but the blindfold had prevented the wood fragments from doing more serious damage.

"Hey, Fletch!" Gann called. "Can you still hear me?"

"Loud and clear, Pappy. Sorry if that disappoints you."

"I'll give you ten seconds to start coming out. One at a time, backward. Otherwise, we'll come after you, blasting."

"You do that," Fletch dared him. "We've got a blaster of our own. Timmy brought it with her."

There was a silence during which he guessed that Gann was inventorying the guerrillas' weapons. His count apparently convinced him that the threat was an empty one. "Good try, Fletch, but the way I make it, all you've got are your bare hands, and maybe a knife. That's not enough and you know it."

"It was enough for Injun. First man through the door gets what he got. Who's going to lead the charge?" Fletch laughed. "Let me guess. It's got to be either Rufus or Choogle, right? They're expendable—like Blossom—

and you're not."

His words were calculated to sow dissension. Perhaps they succeeded. There was another silence. When Gann spoke again, his tone was conciliatory. "Us fighting each other doesn't make sense, Fletch. I've got no real quarrel with you. Maybe we can reach an understanding."

Fletch pointed to the shallow pit and told Moran in a whisper, "See what's down there." Houses were required to have crawl holes. While this ancient structure conformed to no building code, there might be a break in the foundation large enough to permit escape. In a louder voice, he replied, "I'm listening, Pappy."

"Moran's the one I want. Give him to me and you can beat it."

"Timmy too?"

"Timmy too. I don't have any further use for her."

Too quick, Fletch thought, and too easy. However, he allowed Gann to believe that he was sniffing the bait. "How do I know you're on the level?"

"I don't suppose my word of honor would mean anything to you, would it?" Gann did not wait for an answer. "Okay, how does this strike you? You turn over the mayor and we'll clear out in your bus. Then you and Timmy can leave whenever you like."

"Aren't you afraid we'll go to the police?" He kept his eyes fixed on the hole in the floor. What was Moran doing, anyway?

"You won't go to the police," Gann replied confidently. "Timmy's in this as deep as the rest of us. The only way you can save her is by keeping your mouth shut."

Moran's head popped up with the suddenness of a jack-in-the-box. His face was draped with cobwebs and gray with dust but neither concealed his scowl. He had not found the hoped-for exit. All his reconnaissance had uncovered was another weapon of a sort, an empty wine bottle, which he clutched like a club.

"Well, how about it?" Gann demanded.

"Let me get this straight," Fletch parried to buy a little more time, although he could not conceive of a use to put it to. "If I agree to turn the mayor over to you, you agree to leave Timmy and me alone—right?"

"How many times do I have to say it, anyhow?"

"Two for one," Moran muttered. "Maybe you'd better take it."

"You should know better than to believe campaign promises. He doesn't mean to let any of us go, any more than I mean to let him go." Fletch raised his voice again. "Can't say I care for your terms, Pappy. Now you listen to mine. Unconditional surrender. I've already been to the cops. I told the FBI the whole story. You're in a trap."

"Sure we are," Gann scoffed. "Who do you think you're hyping, chum? If you'd told the FBI anything, they'd be here instead of you."

"They are here. The house is surrounded, Pappy. They just agreed to give me first crack at you."

Gann laughed, an expression of contempt rather than mirth. "That's really not up to your standard, Fletch."

"Call me by my rightful name." No matter what the cost, he wanted the satisfaction of hurling the truth in his enemy's face. "It's Fletcher Orr. I'm Curt Orr's brother. You should remember Curt—you stuck him in front of a train."

He heard Timmy's astonished gasp behind him. Gann, on the other side of the door, appeared as startled as she. "Well, well," he said slowly. "So that's what it's all about, huh? Okay, I guess I'll have to give you the same treatment I gave your brother."

"Why didn't you tell me?" Timmy demanded in a reproachful whisper. "Oh, Fletch, if I'd only known! If you'd only trusted me—"

He gazed at her bleakly. "You were on the other side, Timmy. Even after I fell in love with you, I couldn't forget that."

"I was never on their side," she told him. "I was just too stupid to know where I really belonged—and now it's too late."

"Maybe not." He listened intently; another conversation, equally muted, was taking place in the parlor. "Checking their signals," he decided. "They'll be blitzing through that door before long."

Moran responded with the infantryman's sardonic salute to an incoming barrage. "For that which we are about to receive . . ."

"I know a better line than that. It is more blessed to give than to receive. I'll take your bottle, Mayor." Kneeling, he removed the cap from the lantern's fuel tank and poured what remained of the kerosene into the bottle, stoppering it with his handkerchief. He brandished the Molotov cocktail triumphantly. "You two take cover. Get down in the hole."

"What have you got in mind?" Moran asked tensely.

"The dynamite." Fletch groped in his pocket for matches. The tattered folder contained only one; he lit it. "If I can hit it with this—"

"No!" Timmy protested, seizing his arm. "I won't let you! They'll kill you before you can—"

He threw her off. "Do what I say! I don't have time to argue about it. This is my last match, damn it!"

He thought she would obey. But as he touched flame to the wick, watched it ignite and then flare brightly, Timmy seized the bottle from his grasp. Holding the incendiary grenade aloft, she plunged through the door, arm cocked like a quarterback preparing to pass.

Fletch's frantic tackle missed. He saw the deadly bottle leave her fingers, glimpsed Lionel Gann's startled face . . . After that, he was conscious only of sounds. They came in quick succession, almost overlapping: The blast of a shotgun that was drowned by the thunderclap of the crude bomb—which in turn was dwarfed by an awesome explosion which seemed to tear the world apart.

Something struck him in the face with stunning force. Even as he fell, he realized with vague surprise that it was a boot and that it still contained a human foot. That wasn't right somehow. Feet were supposed to be attached to legs . . . A second and more crushing blow erased his bewilderment along with all else as the roof toppled in upon him.

# Eighteen

WHEN HE AWOKE, he was beneath another kind of roof. He stared at the unfamiliar white ceiling for a long while until his sedated mind comprehended at last that he was in a hospital. Am I sick? he wondered. There was a loud ringing in his ears and he couldn't turn his head or move his legs. When he touched his body, his fingers encountered not flesh but unyielding plaster. Suddenly it all came back to him in a rush of vivid horror. "Timmy!" he called hoarsely. "Where are you?"

None of those who responded to his cry was the one he sought. The occasional doctor and the ever-present nurses viewed him with compassion and treated him with skill, replaced his blood and eased his pain—but either could not or would not answer his question.

It seemed like days—and yet it might have only been hours; in his drugged condition he was not sure—until he finally found the person who could. He became aware of a new presence beside his bed and saw Nicholas Vitullo gazing down at him. "How do you feel?" the FBI agent inquired.

"Where the hell have you been?" Fletch whispered.

"Waiting for you to come off the critical list. They tell me you've got a broken neck, among a lot of other jolly things. They also tell me you may get over it if you're lucky—and I guess you've already proved you are."

"Never mind me. What about—"

"Oh, Moran's all right," Vitullo said quickly. "A bit bruised and battered but nothing serious."

And so, ultimately, the question was superfluous; by evading it, Vitullo had already answered it. Still, Fletch's lips formed the name.

Vitullo looked away. "I'm sorry," he murmured. "That dynamite . . . There was barely enough left of Gann and his people to identify."

Anger mingled with his despair. "She wasn't one of Gann's people!"

"You're right. After what she did, there can hardly be any doubt about that." Vitullo sighed. "I wish I had something better than sympathy to offer you. But I can't even give you the recognition you deserve. Washington has clamped the lid down tight on the whole story. The official rationale is that the less we publicize this sort of thing, the less we invite others to try the same game. It's probably a wise move. Certain types of crimes are highly contagious even when they fail—take skyjacking, for instance—and I don't have to tell you how close this one came to succeeding."

"Beautiful," Fletch said bleakly. "All those people dead —and the world won't even know why."

"That's about it, I'm afraid." But the notion did not really distress him; Vitullo was a pragmatic man. "Well, I've got to be running along. Glad to see you're doing okay. If there's anything I can do for you—"

"There's nothing anybody can do." He closed his eyes, wishing only to be left alone with his grief. The next time he opened them, Vitullo was gone and Fletch never saw him again.

During the following days, he had other visitors. Captain Deacon dropped by, full of gruff cheer, bringing him candy and congratulations, neither of which was he able to swallow. General Sugarman's successor at COIN, a brisk and bouncy man named Zimmer, younger than Sugarman but like him a retired officer, called upon him. Zimmer brought no candy but offered him a well-paying executive post with the organization. Yet he did not seem overly disappointed when Fletch refused it. Debts of gratitude are frequently a nuisance, particularly when contracted by one's predecessor.

And late one evening, past visiting hours, Ansel Towne appeared, drawn perhaps by a morbid compulsion to hear the story from the lips of the only one who could tell it all. However, it was Towne who did most of the talking. He spoke not of Timmy's death but of her life—painting her as a happy, sunny-natured girl, a daughter both loved and loving. Fletch knew the truth to be otherwise and he suspected the older man did also, but Towne could not bring himself to admit it. Only when he was on the point of departing did Towne reveal a brief glimpse of his inner torment.

"What went wrong?" he asked hesitantly. "Was it—my fault?"

He was tempted to reply with a curt "yes." His desire to fix the blame was strong. But who was he to judge, much less condemn? "You'll have to answer that question for yourself, Mr. Towne. I simply don't know."

Towne promised to return. But he did not, nor was Fletch surprised; they shared nothing but a common wound and wounds do not heal by constantly reopening them. He learned that Towne had insisted upon paying his medical expenses. Fletch did not object. He lacked funds of his own and he realized that Ansel Towne was seeking to expiate his guilt in the only way he knew.

Of all who made the pilgrimage to his bedside, Otis Moran was the only one to provide real comfort. He came frequently to the hospital, alibiing that "Hell, it's practically on my way home." The tough-souled little mayor was genuinely concerned for his health, emotional as well as physical. While he encouraged him to speak freely of the past, he also insisted that Fletch turn his thoughts to the future.

"A man's got to bury his dead," Moran told him. "You'll be getting out of here in a few weeks. You'll need a job. Got anything lined up?"

"Not really. Show biz is the only thing I know—but I can't say I'm too jazzed about going back to it. The feeling's probably mutual, too."

"Well, chew on this. I'm running for governor next year and people who should know tell me I might even win. I could use a man like you. The youth vote is getting more important all the time. Some politicians are afraid of the young people. I suppose I should be too, after what happened, but I'm not. I'd like to see them brought into the political mainstream, turn them on to casting ballots instead of throwing bombs. I think you could help me do that."

Fletch shook his head as much as the cast would permit. When Moran demanded a reason, he said, "You told me once that the guerrillas didn't understand the Establishment. That's true—but the Establishment doesn't understand the guerrillas, either. You look at their rebellion as a political problem. Sugarman saw it as a military problem. To Vitullo and Deacon, it's a police problem. I guess it's all three, but it's something more, too. Damn it, Mayor, like it or not, those are your children! Forget the crazies like Gann or the animals like Injun. They can't be reached and they can't be saved. I'm talking about the ones who can. The Blossoms and the Choogles and Rufus Wrens— most of all, the Timmys. They're crying and nobody really knows why. I'm not sure they even know themselves. But unless we're all willing to just go on killing each other, somebody had better start finding out and—" He broke off with a sheepish grin. "Forgive the lecture. I haven't been well."

"I think," Moran said slowly, "that you do have a job lined up for yourself, after all. A hell of a big job."

"Oh, I just talk a good fight. I'm a con artist, the world's greatest. If I had to get down to cases, I wouldn't know where to begin."

"You care—and that's where it all begins. Take it from there. I can't tell you how. Lecture, teach, write a book, make a film, set up a mission or form a new party —maybe do nothing except *listen*. You've got one big advantage. You know both sides of the fence. You may be the one who can tear that fence down. Or you may end up crucified on it. Either way, you'll be in damn good company. Think about that."

In the weeks that followed Fletch did little else. At first, he continued to recoil from the crusade Moran proposed. The enormity of the task and its probable futility appalled him. Yet gradually why me? became yes, me. For Curt's sake, he had pursued a bloody vengeance and found it hollow. For Timmy's sake—and for the sake of other Timmys he would never know—he must seek something better.

It was a warm summer morning when he finally left the hospital, still unsteady of gait but sure of purpose. There was a small park across the street from the hospital. He had spent long hours at his window, staring at it. Now, since he had a goal but no immediate destination, he wandered through it as if waiting for someone to join him. And, finally, it seemed to him that someone had and that, whatever the future held, he would never be truly alone.

Three children, girls no older than seven or eight, were playing jump rope on the lawn. He paused to watch them and to listen to their singsong chant. They became aware of his presence and, doubtless warned by their mothers to beware of strange men, broke off the game.

"Don't stop," he told them. "Do you know the one that begins 'On the mountain stands a lady'?"

They regarded him shyly. "Uh-huh," one finally admitted. "Do you know it too?"

"Yeah," Fletch said. "I'm afraid I do."